Murder
in the Stars

Also by
JOHN CREASEY

THREE FOR ADVENTURE
FOUR FIND DANGER
TWO MEET TROUBLE
HEIR TO MURDER
MURDER COMES HOME
WHO SAW HIM DIE?
MURDER BY THE WAY
FOUL PLAY SUSPECTED
WHO DIED AT THE GRANGE ⸮
FIVE TO KILL
MURDER AT KING'S KITCHEN
WHO SAID MURDER?
CRIME WITH MANY VOICES
NO CRIME MORE CRUEL
MURDER MAKES MURDER
MYSTERY MOTIVE
FIRST A MURDER
LEND A HAND TO MURDER
NO END TO DANGER
WHO KILLED REBECCA?
THE DYING WITNESSES
MURDER WEEK-END
DINE WITH MURDER
QUARREL WITH MURDER
TAKE A BODY
LAME DOG MURDER

A Falcon's Head Mystery

Murder
in the Stars
John Creasey

WORLD PUBLISHING
TIMES MIRROR
NEW YORK

Published by The World Publishing Company
Published simultaneously in Canada
by Nelson, Foster & Scott Ltd.

First American edition
First printing—1972

First published in Great Britain in 1953
All rights reserved
ISBN 0–529–04483–8
Library of Congress catalog card number: 70–185116
Printed in the United States of America

WORLD PUBLISHING
TIMES MIRROR

CONTENTS

1. Goldilocks   7
2. A Job for Prince   14
3. Two Ladies   21
4. Killer?   28
5. Morning   34
6. Tale of Murder   41
7. Meeting-place   46
8. Richard   54
9. Wimple Talks   61
10. Man of Action   67
11. The Star-gazer   75
12. High Hand   81
13. Eavesdropping   88
14. Sanctuary   94
15. The Fane Family   101
16. "Bring 'Em All"   108
17. Night Watch   115
18. Night Talk   122
19. Triumph for Richard   127
20. Fraser's Report   134

21. Bad for Richard?   140

22. Grenfell Backs Out 147

23. Fraser Comes Home 154

24. Give Away   161

25. No Slippy   168

26. Family Quarrel   175

27. Life and Death   181

1

MARTIN FANE, strong face set in lines of concentration, sat alone in his office at Quill House in the Strand. A single lamp poured white light on to the desk, showing his hands, pencil, the papers he was studying, a pipe, ash-tray, and half a telephone; everything else was in the shade beyond the bright radius.

The office was silent.

Another light shone in the main outer office, showing the single word and the crown, painted black, on frosted glass. The word was PRINCE. Nothing indicated the business, the casual caller and the passer-by received no help from the word or crown; yet, in their way, they were national possessions.

It was nearly half-past seven, on a March evening. The window overlooked a narrow, ill-lit side street, although it was near enough to the Strand for the traffic noises of London to float in. The noises were fading, the Strand was quiet after the theatres had filled, and would remain so until the theatres emptied.

A door banged, and Martin Fane looked up. Footsteps sounded loud on bare boards. The look of concentration faded, and Martin smiled, pushed the papers away, put the pencil down, and picked up the pipe. The footsteps drew nearer—of a man, running. The outer office door burst open, and the man called:

" Scoop! She's nearly here! "

Martin Fane, called Scoop by his brother and family, saw a shadow appear in the doorway. His brother slowed down.

" Why the blazes are you sitting like a floodlit Buddha? " he demanded. " Can't see a thing out here." He groped for and pressed the light switch down; a fluorescent strip began to flicker. " The trouble with you," he announced, " is antiquarianism, or whatever the word is. Out-dated and out-moded. Why strain your eyes when you can have light as good as daylight? "

" That's only one of the troubles with me," said Martin.

7

" You never said a truer word ! "

The light was fully on now, and showed Richard Fane. He had a figure made for clothes, looked well in whatever he wore, had enormous blue eyes in a face which no one thought of calling handsome, but which had remarkable charm. His ears stuck out, and somehow added to the charm. His hair, light brown, was inclined to curl, and although often ruffled, as now, seldom looked untidy.

He studied his brother for a few seconds, frowning ; then the frown cleared.

" In two minutes she'll be here, and my, is she—— "

" You're probably wrong. She either won't come, or will come in a car or cab and draw up outside the front door."

" My boy," said Richard, " you're wrong. I could tell by the way she walked and the look in her eyes."

" How near did you get ? "

" Well, the look on her face," corrected Richard glibly. " Listen, Scoop, we want the business. Don't turn it down, whatever it is. And if you could get fifty or a hundred in advance, I could use a bit. Say a tenner. Run short, just lately, you know how it is."

" I know exactly how it is," said Martin, and touched the papers in front of him. " You're fifty-five pounds overdrawn."

" Never ! "

" Fact."

" Must be something wrong in the figures." Richard wrinkled his nose. " I knew I was a few pounds down, but not as much as that. Doesn't make any difference, anyhow, we need a nice profitable case. Her clothes are from Paris, or I miss my guess, she looks like a million pounds. And her hair—it's probably made of gold."

" You'd better pull a few strands out," said Martin. " It's the only way you'll ever make any money. I wanted a word with you, serious—— "

A door banged ; the same door, downstairs, which had a hydraulic fitting in need of repair.

" Here she is ! " Richard snatched a comb from his hip pocket and ran it through his hair. " I'll be in the outer office and take the first blow. Then I'll build you up, and bring her in. This may be the break we've been looking for." He moved to the door, hand raised and fore and middle fingers crossed, and disappeared.

Martin's smile had an edge to it.

No one, seeing them together, would guess that they were brothers. Martin was a bigger man; tall, broad and thick-set, and powerful with it. His hair was straight and brushed flat off a broad forehead; he was handsome enough, with calm grey eyes. His chief fault was worrying about his brother's fecklessness.

They had been together in the office of *Prince Investigations* when a woman had telephoned, early in the afternoon. She had sounded young, had certainly been agitated, and had wanted an appointment with " Prince " for half-past seven that evening. Martin had made the appointment. They had gone out for a late tea, returned about seven, and Richard had decided to wait outside and get a first view of the caller.

Footsteps sounded on the stairs, quieter, less flurried than Richard's; he had left the outer door ajar. Martin could imagine him sitting at the desk in the outer office, papers spread out, telephone at hand.

There was a tap.

" Come in ! " called Richard.

Martin stood up and went to the door, standing so that he could see out without being seen.

The outer door opened and a girl came in. She didn't look much more than twenty. She was bare-headed, and her hair looked like spun gold. She wore an afternoon dress which had indefinable quality, and a mink wrap. The light glittered on a brooch; only diamonds scintillated so brilliantly. She was small, moved with grace, and gave the impression of being highly strung.

Richard smiled; socially, his smile was worth a fortune.

" Good evening. Can I—— "

" Are you Prince ? "

" I'm one of the partners—— "

" I don't want to see a partner, I want to see Prince."

" And you shall," said Richard. " I'll take you into the great man himself in a few minutes. You did ring up this afternoon, didn't you ? "

" Yes," said the girl. Her gaze roamed.

Martin moved away from the door, to his desk.

"You forgot to give your name," Richard said. "If you'll—— "

She turned away from him and went straight to Martin's door, seeing the light on. Richard said, "Here!" and might as well have kept quiet. The girl thrust the door open as Martin settled in his chair and tried to look as if he had been sitting there all the time.

"Are you *Prince*?" She drew nearer, and was almost accusing.

"Yes," said Martin. "Sit down." He waved to a chair and picked up several papers, straightened them and put them under a stone which served as paper-weight. He didn't look at the girl—or at Richard, hovering in the doorway.

The girl hesitated, then took a chair. She sat on the edge, tensely. If her manner were any indication, she was used to men doing exactly what she wanted, and found Martin's casualness strange enough to be startling. He finished with the papers, picked up a blank white card and a pencil, looked at her, and spoke without smiling.

"I have to be frank, from the beginning. There are certain cases which don't interest me. Divorce cases, for instance. Some other cases have to be referred to the police, and we use our own discretion, are not necessarily guided by the client's wishes."

Richard was making faces at him, and the girl stared as if at some strange animal.

"I'm sure that's clear," Martin said.

She leaned farther forward on the chair, and breathed, "*Are* you Prince?"

Martin picked up his pipe and tobacco-pouch and began to fill the bowl; he had broad hands with rather short fingers, not stubby, and very powerful.

"I don't quite know what you expect," he said. "There isn't such a man as Prince. My father, a writer of mystery stories, has created a character called Prince, and a lot of people know of him. This agency, which I run with my brother, has taken the character's name. I am the senior partner, my brother is the junior partner. We'll both do all we can to help you—within the limits I've mentioned."

"Oh," she said.

Richard threw up his hands, and then buried his face in them. He turned away from the door in an attitude of utter dejection. The girl sat quite still; it was impossible to judge whether she was disappointed or just mildly shocked.

Martin lit his pipe.

" Now ! What's the trouble ? "

" I'm terrified about my mother," said the girl.

A year in this office had brought Martin many odd characters with as many strange stories, and he was gradually learning to judge who were a little wrong in the head. He didn't think this girl was, but he didn't trust her. He frowned.

" I see." He was very matter of fact. " Why ? "

A gurgling noise came from the outer office.

" She's being threatened with murder," said the girl. " I really am terrified. We were together for luncheon on Monday, she went to do some shopping, was back late. I nearly called the police."

Martin's expression remained blank.

" Why didn't you ? " he asked.

" I *can't* go to the police. I don't know what it's about, only—she's really frightened. She quarrels with me, with every one for that matter, and——— "

" Any one in particular ? " Martin asked.

The girl sat so far on the edge of the chair that she looked in imminent danger of falling off. No one could mistake her tension; the difficulty was to be sure what caused it. Her eyes were big and cornflower blue; more blue than Richard's. She was well made up, but not beautiful; she'd made the best of a reasonable job by Mother Nature. She had a kind of shrewdness, which her manner nearly concealed.

" Well, yes, I suppose so. She's quarrelled a lot with my uncle—my father's brother, that is. Father's dead, and— but all this doesn't matter now."

" If she's frightened of being murdered by someone, she would quarrel with anyone she suspected," said Martin mildly.

" Oh, she doesn't suspect *him*. I don't think she suspects anyone, but she won't tell me anything. Well, hardly anything. Please will you help ? "

" Does your mother know you're consulting us ? "

" No ! And she mustn't know, she—— "

" I'm sorry," said Martin, " but I'm afraid I can't help you."

He knew that Richard would condemn the tactics, but decided that they were best. The girl wasn't telling him all she could, and obviously didn't mean to ; he couldn't explain why he was sure of that, he simply was. If she really needed help she might change her mind in the face of that blunt refusal.

She looked flabbergasted, then glanced quickly down to her handbag, opened it, and began to fumble inside. " I can pay your fee, I've plenty of money here." She drew out a wad of one-pound notes.

So she thought money could buy everything.

" Listen," said Martin, standing in front of her and resting a hand on her shoulder. " Go back and see your mother, tell her what you're doing, and say that if she wants my help, I'll have to see her. I must have the whole story— why she won't go to the police, for instance. I'll keep anything confidential, and I'll try to help if she's really in trouble, but I can't start work with half a story."

The girl sat as if stunned ; but he thought that was partly an act. That was why he had been so brusque ; he wasn't convinced that she was as frightened as she tried to make out.

" My brother will see you home, and you can have a chat with your mother," said Martin. " By the way, what's your name ? "

She didn't answer. Martin shrugged and went to the door—then stopped abruptly. Richard wasn't there. Richard believed in taking whatever offered, without pausing to think, and was desperately anxious to lift Prince Investigations out of the slough of financial depression which had snared it during the past few months. Richard had probably gone home, disgusted.

Martin turned from the door. The girl hadn't moved. He hoped that his tactics would make her tell the truth, but she hadn't yet reached a decision. As he moved towards her, he smiled and said :

" I'll see you home, if—— "

" No." She jumped up. " I don't need you ! "

She looked at him searingly; and he had an uneasy feeling that she was badly frightened and that he was wrong not to have been more cautious. The trouble was that he thought she was lying—or at least trying to fool him. She rushed past him, clutching the bag, which was still open; it was a large one, and the wad of notes was probably two or three hundred pounds. He opened the door for her, and she flew across the outer office, reached that door first, and ran out.

He followed quickly, leaving the lights on.

He was in the street ten yards behind her as she ran towards the Strand, only thirty yards away. She fled round the corner, watched curiously by several passers-by. As he rounded the corner he saw a powerful car drawn into the side of the road, with a chauffeur standing beside it. A few yards behind, Richard sat at the wheel of their jointly owned Buick; he pretended not to see Martin.

Martin grinned, turned back into the side street, waited until the two cars had driven off, and actually chuckled as he re-entered the building. Richard had guessed what would happen, but was determined to be in the hunt; Richard had hunches which were surprisingly often right. Martin lost his uneasy feeling as he hurried up the stairs. These led from the side entrance of Quill House; the main entrance was being repaired and hadn't been in use for nearly two months.

He turned into the office.

He didn't go straight across to his own, but paused, then went to Richard's desk—actually the receptionist's, but used by Richard that evening. He wasn't interested in the desk, but wanted time to think.

He'd heard a movement in his office.

It certainly wasn't Richard; it might be someone who had a right there, but he didn't think that likely He made up his mind, pushed his forefinger against the inside of his coat pocket, gun-fashion, and then walked briskly towards the open door.

A middle-aged man sat at his desk, smiling at him.

2

A JOB FOR PRINCE

MARTIN took his hand away from his pocket as soon as he saw the man. No danger threatened here. He drew out his pipe and stuck it between his lips, nodded, and approached the desk slowly.

" Good evening," he greeted.

" Good evening, Mr. Fane."

" I don't usually see people as late as this."

" I'm sure you'll agree that this is an exceptional night," the other said.

There was laughter in his voice. He was probably older than he looked; his complexion was good, his skin fresh, and his hair, crisp and inclined to curl, was greying at the temples. He had clear, grey eyes and well-defined eyebrows. He wore a dinner jacket, and had Richard's way of wearing clothes as if he had been made for them. Handsome wasn't quite the word for him. Distinguished? His voice was pleasant and not affected.

Martin said, " No, it isn't really exceptional. I sometimes have late appointments."

The man chuckled.

" Not with young women like my niece. Tell me how you managed to get rid of her so quickly. If she was determined to make you work for her, and she usually gets her own way, what drove her off? "

" So you have a niece." Martin pulled up another chair and sat down.

This was a much more comfortable chair, with padded seat and sides, and meant for favoured clients; all clients were favoured when they first came. He was thinking that the girl hadn't shown much enthusiasm for her uncle; and had said that her mother was always quarrelling with him. Was this the same uncle?

" She came to see you," said his visitor. " I caught sight of her leaving."

Martin shrugged. " Did you ? "

The other frowned, leaned back in his chair, and took out a slim gold cigarette-case. He made a great show of opening

it, drawing attention to his well-manicured nails and pale, well-kept hands. He lit his cigarette before he said slowly :
" Aren't you being a little difficult ? "
" Am I ? " asked Martin, as if it were a new thought. " I don't know. I thought I'd finished work for the day, and I'm tired. I never like dealing with burglars, anyhow. If you tell me that I left the door open, it might be true, but the police would take a lot of convincing if I were to say it was locked before you arrived. Wouldn't they ? "
" I see your point." The other smiled. " But I think we can get round this without resorting to the police—that's if you're anything of the man your father is."
" Do you know him ? "
" We're acquainted. I think he would acknowledge me," said the visitor. " My name is Grenfell—Sir Edward Grenfell."
Martin kept a poker-face. The name meant something ; he couldn't recall what, for the time being ; that would come. Meanwhile, his tactics must be to keep the other talking. Just as the girl had obviously been well-off, so was the man ; if outward appearances had anything to commend them.
" My niece," said Grenfell, " is Miss Rhoda Grenfell—the only child of my only brother, Sydney. He died some years ago. I've often been foolish enough to disapprove of her ideas, and try to make her behave less foolishly. She's twenty-five, old enough to be sensible. Unfortunately her mother encourages her in her foolish spending, and I'm consequently an unpopular adviser. They listen to someone else, though."
Martin's poker-face remained unchanged.
" Now she and her mother are in some kind of trouble and won't confide in me," said Grenfell. " Did she confide in you ? " He paused hopefully, but went on again quickly, " I doubt if she was here long enough. You may as well admit that she was here, Mr. Fane, because I really saw her go. I was outside when she arrived, on the landing outside here when your brother came out, and downstairs in the hall when you followed him, after Rhoda. Instead of waiting for you downstairs I came up here."
" Very interesting," said Martin. " You say her name is Rhoda Grenfell."

"Didn't she give her name?" Grenfell looked surprised, then amused. "I must say there are times when she looks as if she has her head screwed on the right way! She's no fool." He began to frown. "I wish I knew what the trouble is. I've a nasty feeling that it's all caused by a fortune-teller. An astrologer, but I may be wrong. Care to find out for me?"

"I don't like wasting my time," said Martin.

Grenfell said, "I don't think it will be a waste of time."

There was a change in his manner, hard to define but undoubtedly there. Martin judged that he had stalled enough, and that Grenfell would lose patience if he stalled any more. He'd placed the man now; Grenfell, of the *Sunday Clarion*. The *Sunday Clarion* was an independent newspaper—independent, that was, of any of the big groups—which had a mammoth circulation. That in itself made both visits of exceptional interest; Richard would call it the greatest slice of luck they'd had.

"You never know," said Martin. "The most promising cases flop." He smiled. He hadn't the charm of Richard, but when he smiled there was something extremely attractive about him. "With anyone else, I'd play canny a bit longer, but I recognise you, of course—and you wouldn't come here for the sake of a chat. I take it she *was* your niece."

"Oh, yes. More's the pity."

"She looks a credit to you," Martin said.

"Looks is about all." Grenfell shrugged. "Still, I didn't come to talk about Rhoda's limitations, although you need to know what I can tell you about her, if you're going to help. I'll be brief. She and her mother are in some sort of trouble, and it can't be money, as they're both wealthy. I want to find out what it is. I could use one of the *Clarion's* staff, but I haven't a man I particularly want to probe into family affairs. As a private agency, Prince is unique, and in any case I'd trust a son of Jonathan Fane, unless I knew of a reason to distrust him." He smiled. "Is that all satisfactory?"

"Plenty of blarney, but I'll take it," said Martin.

Grenfell laughed.

"You don't exactly go down on your hands and knees and beg for business, do you? I thought you were having a r your impressive launching twelve months

t so ? " Martin asked lazily.

' general inquiries." Grenfell lit another

follow Rhoda here this evening ? "

Rhoda ? " He seemed genuinely surprised. " Of course I didn't. I came to see you—professionally. I've told you why."

" Then the fact that you and Rhoda both chose the same evening was—— "

" Pure coincidence." Grenfell nodded. " Odd, but true. I had no idea she had even heard of you."

" Very odd," agreed Martin drily. " Rhoda had an appointment, of course—but for you this was an odd time to come. Really, you were lucky to find me here. Usually the office is closed long before this time—— "

" I know. It was closed this time yesterday, and the day before."

Martin stared. " You mean—— "

" My dear fellow," interrupted Grenfell, " you don't think I could come during the day, or even ring up for an appointment, when I wanted to keep it secret, do you ? With Fleet Street only a stone's throw away—why, I might just as well have announced my intentions on the front page of the *Clarion*. Of course I had to come late, and just hope to catch you in one evening. Third time was lucky—thanks, it seems, to Rhoda."

" I see," said Martin woodenly. " What do you want me to do ? "

" I want you to find out what's troubling my niece. I think this fortune-teller is at the back of it—a woman named Hilda Kennedy. I want you to find out all you can about her. I'll pay a reasonable fee and expenses. What do you call a reasonable fee ? "

Martin said promptly, " A hundred pounds a week."

" All right. Like the first cheque now ? "

" When you like, preferably within a week," said Martin, and wondered what Richard would say to that. He sat puffing at his pipe and watching the older man, and wondering whether Grenfell was nearer fifty than forty. Grenfell

was obviously waiting for him to speak. Martin said,
" What else can you tell me ? "

" I've told you everything I know."

Martin looked sceptical.

" Oh, that's true," said Grenfell. " There's no point in
lying about it. There may be a scandal. If there is, I've
no knowledge. Rhoda and her mother and I have never
been really close friends. Since Rhoda started throwing
money away, gambling wildly and that kind of thing, I've
protested—as I've told you. We're now on formal terms.
Mutual friends have told me that they've been showing signs
of strain lately, and I faced them with it this morning. I was
flatly told to mind my own business, by both of them—in fact
everything confirmed that they are worried. Don't you
agree about Rhoda ? "

" Yes. She came with half a story, and I tried shock
tactics. They didn't work."

Grenfell shrugged.

" You know your business best, but if she comes back, I
hope you'll try to get the truth from her. What happened exactly ? "

" I told her to go away and think it over and come again if
she were prepared to tell me the whole truth."

Grenfell whistled.

" Straight talk, for Rhoda ! She probably hasn't got over
the shock yet. As a matter of fact, Mr. Fane, she has too
many good-looking young men to her bow. The trouble
might have something to do with one of them. That's
simply a guess. Her father spoiled her, and her mother
isn't very strong on discipline. Do you know her ? "

" No."

" I'll give you any information you expect to find useful,"
said Grenfell. " I'd rather you didn't come to see me, and
keep in touch by telephone. Use your own name, but not
that of Prince." He stood up, slowly ; and startled Martin
by his height ; he was well over six feet, but sitting, had
seemed a much shorter man. " What makes you think that
she might come back ? "

Martin shrugged.

" I hope the hunch is right." Grenfell moved towards
the door. " I must say I admired the way in which your

brother got to work. You'll impress upon him the need for
secrecy for the time being, won't you ? And I'm relying on
you to report to me if anything should transpire which looks
as if it ought to be dealt with by anyone else."

"If I think it's a police job, I'll tell you," Martin
promised.

"Obviously I needn't ask you to call a spade a spade !"
They were at the outer office, and Grenfell shook hands.
"Let me know something as soon as you can. Good night.
You needn't see me downstairs."

He turned and hurried off, giving Martin the impression
that he was more worried than he had made out, and that he
wanted to be on his own. His footsteps were swift as he
went downstairs; they seemed to slacken when he neared
the door. Soon it slammed. Martin rubbed his chin, drew
at his empty pipe, and went back to the smaller office. He
spent five minutes looking through the accounts, on which
he had been working when the girl had come; he was a
believer in letting new facts settle before trying to sift them.
He tidied up, locked everything away, and glanced at his
watch; it was half-past eight. He doubted whether Richard
would come back here; their flat was only five minutes' walk
away. He locked up and went downstairs. He was in the
street, buttoning his coat against a gust of cold wind from the
Strand, before he let himself think about Grenfell.

Had the newspaper owner lied ? Had he protested too
much that he was telling the whole truth ? If he had told
Martin everything he knew, was there any sufficient reason
for coming to Prince in preference to using one of his own
staff ? Above all, why had he come on the same evening—
almost at the same time—as Rhoda ? His suggestion that it
was a pure coincidence seemed incredible; and yet, Martin
reasoned, Grenfell had had no need to come immediately
after Rhoda. If he had followed her, he could have gone
away again and paid a visit a few days later, when it would
not have seemed quite so obvious. Unless, of course, he
had acted on impulse. But he did not seem the sort of man
to act on impulse. The only other possible explanation
seemed to be that the matter was urgent and speed was
necessary. But why——

Martin turned two corners before reaching Maiden Lane.

This was a short, narrow street at the back of the Strand. Publishing houses and exporters held most of the premises, there was a fashionable restaurant, not open at night, on one side; almost opposite was a grocer's shop and café combined. The Fanes' flat was above this. Martin unlocked the door, after a glance up to the darkened front room; Richard wasn't back. He pushed the door behind him, the wind caught it, and it slammed; all doors seemed to slam to-night. He went up one flight of bare wooden stairs and past a suite of offices; then up a carpeted flight to his own place.

This had been boarded off from the landing, making the flat completely self-contained. There were three rooms—two small bedrooms, one little more than a cubicle, and a living-cum-dining-room-cum-study. The kitchen and bathroom were on one level, the other rooms were approached by a short flight of steps.

Martin went up these in the dark, switched on a light, and looked about the big room. It was pleasantly furnished; most of the homely and yet artistic touches came from his mother, others from his fiancée. Barbara, who worked with Prince, had been down with 'flu and, if he had his way, wouldn't return to the office for at least another week. His parents were at their Dorset home.

He turned from the main part of the room to a dining-alcove, lined with books. In one corner was a small desk. Officially it was shared; actually, he used it much more than Richard. He was worried about Richard, and was detached enough to sit back and remind himself that he always had been. Richard's money troubles, Richard's love affairs, Richard's enthusiasms. Richard took success well, failure poorly; not that he was a bad loser, but a succession of failures dispirited him. He was getting depressed about a run of bad luck at Prince. The agency had started with a sensational success, but for three months nothing that really brought in any money had come along. Richard had regarded the mysterious telephone call as the turning of the tide.

He could be right.

Martin sat at the desk, but couldn't settle; he wouldn't, until Richard came back to report. Richard's jaunt had probably been a failure; on the other hand, he might come in excitedly, to announce that the unnamed girl was none other than——

The telephone bell rang.

Martin was on the other side of the room from the instrument. He hurried across and snatched up the receiver.

" Martin Fane speaking."

" Who is that ? "   A woman spoke, sharply.   " Did you say you were Martin Fane ? "

" That's right."

" Hold on *one* moment," said the woman.

The moment grew into several.   Martin began to fidget, seeing no reason for disquiet, but feeling it.   Then the telephone was picked up at the other end, and he heard Richard. Richard hadn't sounded so glum for months.

" Scoop, old chap."

" Yes."

" Needn't bark my head off," said Richard forlornly. " I'm in a jam.   Held up, by two—er—by two ladies. One's pointing a gun at my head, right now.   Er—do what they ask, won't you, the damned thing might go off."

3   TWO LADIES

MARTIN had no time to answer, for he heard a protest from Richard and guessed that the receiver had been snatched out of his grasp.   Martin began to smile, faintly, the corners of his lips curving and a gleam creeping into his eyes.   He heard a mutter of conversation in the background, followed by the voice he had first heard.

" Did you understand what this man said, Mr. Fane ? "

" Clearly."

" I'm glad you did.   He forced his way into my flat."

" Very silly of him," said Martin gravely.

" Silly isn't the word I would use—I prefer burglary," said the woman tartly.   She wasn't Rhoda Grenfell;   she might be the mother.   " I want to see you at once."

" Where ? "

" Here, of course. I—Rhoda, *don't* keep interrupting. Mr. Fane—Rhoda! I—oh, just a minute."

Voices off sounded again, and Martin just heard Rhoda saying, " *He doesn't know the address.*"

" How could I tell him, with you jumping about all over the place ? "   The woman with the receiver obviously thrust the mouthpiece closer to her lips, for her voice became deafening.   " Come to eighteen Lingham Court, *at once*, Mr. Fane. If you don't, I won't be responsible for what might happen to your brother. *Sit down !* "

Either Rhoda or Richard had annoyed her.

Martin rang off, but didn't move away from the telephone at first ; he was seldom guilty of impulsive action. He stood considering the new element, decided it was mildly amusing, and went to the desk and fingered the telephone directory. Mrs. Sydney Grenfell lived in St. John's Wood ; no one of the name lived at Lingham Court, which was an ostentatious block of luxury flats in Mayfair. His father's publisher had a suite there.

He left his own flat five minutes afterwards and, when Richard would have taken a taxi, walked to the nearest tube station and took a train to Green Park. He walked again from there.

Lingham Court was an immense grey-white block on the corner of two narrow streets. Subdued lights shone over the entrances and from most of the windows ; it looked rather like a factory. The Buick was parked outside. A commissionaire, well-wrapped-up against the cold, came forward, the movement of his hands suggesting that he had been smoking a surreptitious cigarette.

" Help you, sir ? "

" Flat Eighteen, please."

" That's right, sir, this entrance. Miss Kennedy. It's on the first floor, sir, will you take the lift, sir—— "

" I'll walk, thanks."   Grenfell had talked of a Hilda Kennedy—the fortune-telling astrologer.

" Turn right at the top of the stairs, and it's the last door along, you can't miss it."

Martin entered a spacious hall, brightly lit, richly carpeted, and fitted up rather like a miniature hall of mirrors. The staircase led to the right, and the commissionaire, assuming that Martin could do nothing for himself, led him to the foot of it. He hurried up, loosening his coat and taking off his hat. He didn't wear gloves.

The passage to the right of the landing was empty. He strolled along, trying to decide what line to take, and refusing to speculate about Hilda Kennedy. He stopped outside a chromium door and pressed the bell. After a second's pause the door opened. A middle-aged woman, flat-breasted, flat-headed, and dressed absurdly in scarlet, stood with a hand on the door and suspicious eyes staring at him out of a curiously flat face. She was so odd that she didn't seem real.

" Mr. Fane ? " Her voice was familiar, from the telephone call.

" Yes."

" I thought you were never coming," she said impatiently. " Over there." She pointed to a door which stood ajar, and waited for him to go ahead. Her brusqueness wasn't important; but he was beginning to wonder if this was going to be what he expected. He hesitated by the door. " Go on, go in," she called from behind him.

Martin went in.

The girl who had visited him earlier stood near the door, with an automatic pistol in her right hand. She was pointing this at Richard, who sat stiffly on an upright chair, looking miserable and ridiculous.

His feet were bare.

His shoes and socks stood a foot away from him, looking as forlorn as he did himself. His hair was tousled and there was a scratch near his right eye; the scratch had bled slightly.

Martin surveyed him and inwardly rejoiced, but outwardly kept a straight face.

" Mr. Fane," said the woman who had admitted him, " *is* this your brother, Richard ? "

" Yes."

" I've told you—— " Richard began, then lapsed into silence, partly because the girl with the gun moved it upwards, sharply.

Martin had paid her little attention.

"We had to be *sure*," said the flat-chested woman.

"But this young lady saw him earlier to-night."

"Rhoda *thought* she saw him. She was only interested in seeing you, and I must say that you disappointed her very much indeed."

"Sorry," murmured Martin.

"She came away, came *here*, and soon afterwards this young man forced his way into the flat. Rhoda had been so worried and in such a hurry that she forgot to close the door. He sneaked in, and that's *bur*glary. I don't mind admitting that I shall want a full explanation before I'm satisfied. I might go to the police, yet."

"Oh, don't do that," said Martin. "You don't want them to laugh at you." He moved slowly towards Rhoda Grenfell.

"Laugh!" exclaimed the older woman.

"Laugh," repeated Martin solemnly, and shot out his right hand, took the gun, and moved away before Rhoda had realised what had happened.

She gasped. Martin backed towards the corner, and examined the gun.

The flat-chested woman exclaimed, "Put that down!"

"Later," said Martin. "Have you a licence for this?"

Neither of the women answered. Rhoda began to flush; her eyes, which had sparked with anger, became worried. The other woman, presumably Miss Kennedy, tightened lips which were already thin, looked from the girl to Martin, then back accusingly at the girl. Richard was forgotten.

"Rhoda, *have* you a licence?" demanded Miss Kennedy.

"I——"

"*Have you?*"

"Oh, don't keep shouting at me," cried Rhoda Grenfell. "It's all you seem to have done all night, Hilda. I won't have it. No, I haven't a licence for the beastly thing. I didn't know you had to have a licence, and I don't care. I don't feel safe without——"

Hilda Kennedy snapped, "Don't be ridiculous!"

The two women glared at each other, and Richard, who was nothing if not resilient, glanced at Martin and winked; Martin appeared not to notice that.

"I'm not being ridiculous." Rhoda's voice was shrill.

" The way you talk you'd think I was a child, instead of—— "

" From the way you behave you might *be* a child."

" Hilda, if you—— "

" If you would only do what I advise instead of tearing off on foolish errands by yourself, you'd be much happier."

" Oh, shut up ! "

" I won't be spoken to like that," said Hilda Kennedy angrily. " By a chit of a girl who doesn't know what's good for her. If I had my way—— "

" If you don't stop, I'll go now ! "

It wouldn't be long before the girl really lost her temper, and that wasn't simply because of the quarrel. There was more here, much evidence of emotional strain. Martin, looking from one to the other, decided that if this went on, they would get thoroughly out of hand. This was the moment to interrupt.

" Let's get the affair of the pistol straight," he said. " It's an offence to carry firearms without a licence. The offence is much graver if it's loaded, of course." He snapped open the magazine and glanced in ; a fleeting grin crossed his face, but he drove it away quickly. " Still, it's bad enough, empty."

" Empty," groaned Richard.

" At least you had the good sense not to load it, Rhoda," said Hilda Kennedy grudgingly.

" Now let's examine what's happened this evening," said Martin. " This young lady came to me with half a story, and I told her I wanted to know everything. My brother thought that she looked nervous, not to say frightened." He measured his words carefully. " He followed her, came up here, and found the door open. He came in, to make sure that she was all right. It's no crime to enter for that reason, Miss Kennedy."

" How do you know my name ? " the woman snapped.

" I asked the porter." Martin waved as if that weren't important, dropped the gun into his pocket, and turned to face Richard. " We might have a case against them, old chap. How did you get that scratch ? "

Richard gulped. " I—er—— "

" I hit him," said Rhoda Grenfell.

" Oh, I see. Bodily assault—— "

" Don't talk nonsense," said Miss Kennedy. " She had every reason to strike him, and had I been in her place I would have hit him harder."

" And got yourself into more trouble." Martin shrugged. " Well, we'd better forget it. Come on, Richard." He turned towards the door.

Neither of the women moved. Martin didn't look at them, but knew they were staring at each other, questioningly. Richard bent down for his shoes and socks, and put them on slowly ; he didn't tie the shoe laces, but jumped up as if he couldn't put this room behind him quickly enough. Martin, already at the door, seemed to have forgotten the women.

They spoke together.

" Mr. Fane—— " began Rhoda.

" Just a moment—— " started Hilda Kennedy.

Martin turned. " Yes ? "

" We—should like you to help us," Miss Kennedy said weakly. " Miss Grenfell is in great trouble, she really needs help."

" I doubt it. If she did, she would come to me with a complete story. If she decides to tell me the whole truth, I'll gladly see what I can do. To-morrow. I'll be at my office at half-past nine." He nodded and turned away.

Rhoda Grenfell made a mute attempt to call him back, but he pretended not to hear. He walked out, with Richard just behind him. They didn't speak until they reached the hall, and were saluted by the commissionaire.

" Really going ? " asked Richard mildly.

" Of course."

" I'm not sure you're right, Scoop. They're in the mood to spill all the beans now, but when they've slept on it they might feel differently."

" Then if they told us part of the truth to-night and wished they hadn't in the morning, they'd make up something else to smear the trail. If they want us, they can come in the morning." Martin swung towards the car, and Richard climbed in by his side silently. Neither spoke until they reached a parking plot, near the café, where they left the car both day and night.

They got out, in a strained silence.

"After all," said Richard plaintively, "it could have happened to any one."

"Oh, of course. Two-to-one were hopeless odds."

"That's not like you, Scoop." Richard was reproachful. "Never hit a man when he's down. If that wench had caught my eye she might have injured me for life."

"Instead of that she caught you on your vanity, but that won't last a lifetime."

"What the devil's got into you?" demanded Richard, as they walked up the staircase. It was dark, but they were so familiar with every turn and every tread that darkness didn't matter. "I thought I might be able to find out who she was. You could have fixed the job up in the office, if you'd played your cards right. Obviously she was lying, but once you'd started on the job, the truth would have come out, and we should be in the money again. That *is* important, you know."

"Beginning to realise we need some cash, are you?"

"Now look here!" They stopped on the tiny landing outside the front door while Martin fumbled for his keys. "I know I made a crashing fool of myself, but if it had come off I would have discovered that—— "

"Her name is Rhoda Grenfell, her father, Sydney Grenfell, is dead, her mother is scatter-brained, she's a spend-thrift heiress, and her uncle is the owner of the *Sunday Clarion*," said Martin. He could imagine Richard's expression; the darkness took away some of the relish of that mild triumph, but not all.

"That wouldn't be Sir Edward Grenfell, would it?" asked Richard unexpectedly.

Martin paused with the key in the lock.

"Go to the top of the class," he said. "Know him?"

"Of him," answered Richard. "Small world, isn't it?"

Martin turned the key, pushed the door open, and stood aside for Richard to pass. Richard groped for the light-switch, but didn't touch it.

A man said harshly, "Don't put on a light. Stay where you are. I've got a gun."

There was a moment of silence; deep, shattering. Then Martin dropped his right hand towards his pocket and the empty gun—but didn't touch it.   The bright light of a torch shone from behind them ; so there was a man back and front.

The man in the flat said, " Keep your hands in sight and come in, slowly."

4   KILLER ?

MARTIN FANE went slowly forward ; Richard didn't move. Martin thought only of Richard, who was often foolhardy ; if the man in front was a killer, Richard might be killed.

" Move forward, I said."   The voice from the room was harsh and threatening.

The man was just visible, but Richard and Martin cast shadows over him, they couldn't see his face.   By some freak a shaft of light fell on the gun in his right hand ; it didn't waver.

" Don't play the fool," Martin muttered.

The light moved ; the man behind pushed Richard in the small of the back and sent him forward.   Richard caught his foot on the edge of a rug and fell sprawling at the feet of the man with the gun.

" Close the door," this man said.

The door closed with a snap.   Martin looked round ; the second man was inside the room, still shining the torch, which was big and powerful and cut the room into light and shadow.   Richard scrambled to his feet, slipped again, and was within a foot of the gun.   If he did anything crazy, he couldn't be missed.

" Richard ! "   Martin's voice was hoarse with anxiety.

" Not my night out," Richard said.   " I'm not going to try anything."

He moved back a pace—and kicked.   He caught the barrel of the gun, sent it flying out of the man's hand and spinning towards the ceiling.   Martin swung round.   Richard had made the chance, he could use it ; fears faded.   Then Richard, off his balance, staggered into him and sent him forward, helplessly ; both were helpless.   Martin saw the shadowy figure of the man by the door as he moved, then felt a blow on the side of the head, savage, powerful. His head reeled. Another blow caught him behind the ear, and he pitched forward, hit the floor, and lay still; he wasn't unconscious, but the pain was too great for him to move to attack.

Fear for Richard surged back.

He wasn't sure how long he lay there; it must have been several minutes. He began to get up, but a hand was thrust at the back of his head and he was pushed down again. A man pulled at his wrists; he felt cord being tied round them and tightened enough to hurt. Next he was pushed over on his back, his whole weight on his bound wrists and arms; the strain was agonising, and he couldn't do a thing to ease it.

The torchlight shone eerily about the room, and shadows moved. He turned his head, seeking Richard; and saw him lying on the couch, quite still. Martin thought there was a dark patch on Richard's head, another on the light-coloured tapestry of the couch.

Blood ?

The man with the harsh voice pulled up a chair and sat a couple of feet away from Martin. The torch shone fully into Martin's eyes. The strength of the beam of white was so great that it made his eyes water and he couldn't keep them open; they kept flickering, he seemed to have lost control over his eyelids.

The man said, " You'll get hurt more, Fane, if you don't talk. What did the girl tell you ? "

Martin licked his lips. " What—girl ? "

The man shifted his position slightly and kicked him in the ribs; it wasn't hard, just an earnest of what would follow if he were stubborn.

" You know what girl. Rhoda Grenfell. What did she tell you ? "

Martin said, " Nothing I believed."

The foot kicked against his ribs again, harder.

" Don't give me that. What did she say ? "

Martin said, " I can't make you believe me. She said that her mother's frightened of being murdered, and wanted me to help her. She—— "

He paused, for the man caught his breath, as if he were surprised; let him think round that. Martin tried to ease to one side and get his weight off his hands; he felt as if a bone would break.

" Go on."

" That's about all.   I wouldn't play."

" She offered you money, didn't she ? "

" I tell you I wouldn't play.   I can't work for clients who aren't frank with me."

Martin wasn't really concentrating.   The man had moved forward, slightly, allowing another glimpse of Richard, who hadn't moved.   The dark patches on his head and the couch seemed to be larger.   Martin gritted his teeth, felt despairing; if that were a serious head wound, Richard might be bleeding to death.

" How do you know she was keeping anything back ? "

Martin made himself think, managed to keep his watering eyes open and stare into the other's shadowy face.   He couldn't see enough of that face to be helpful later; the light made the eyes shine oddly, made the face look gaunt, like a skeleton.

" I—guessed.   I told her to come back if she wanted to tell me the truth.   That's all."

" So that's all."   The man hesitated, as if he weren't sure whether to believe it or not, turned his head and glanced at the man holding the torch, and said, " What do you make of it, Claude ? "

He'd slipped, using a name.   Claude.   The name burned itself into Martin's mind.   Claude didn't answer immediately, but looked towards Martin.   Neither of them took any notice of Richard—who didn't move and didn't make a sound.   In the pause the silence in the flat seemed like the silence of death.

Claude made a sighing noise, and conceded, " Could be."

The man with the gun turned back to Martin.

" Where did your brother go ? "

So they'd been watching and had seen Richard follow; a lie wouldn't help.

" He—followed her."

" Why, if you weren't going to take the job? "

" I didn't say I wasn't going to take it—if she told the truth.   And if she decided to come and see me again, I wanted to know more about her.   So Richard—what did you do to him ? " He couldn't keep the fear out of his voice.

" Forget it. So Richard what ? "

" Followed her."

" Where to ? "

" Lingham Court."

The man glanced at Claude and took a long time deciding what he was going to ask next. Claude lit a cigarette with one hand ; the flare of the lighter added to the light in the room.

" What did he find out ? "

" Nothing. There were two women there, and they caught him. I went to get him out of the jam."

" All right," said the man with the gun. " Now what did Grenfell say ? "

" He wasn't frank either. He just wanted me to try to find out what was troubling the girl and her mother."

" Nothing else ? "

" Nothing."

The man with the gun stopped asking questions.

" Listen, Fane," he said heavily, " I don't mind about Grenfell, but if that girl goes to see you in the morning, turn her down. Don't even let her talk. Drop the job, see ? Don't do another thing about it, or you won't like what will happen to you."

He stood up, kicked Martin lightly in the ribs again, then turned towards the door. Claude opened it, as if he was glad to be going. They didn't speak to each other or to Martin. The torches shone on the landing, then the light was cut off as the door closed with a snap. Footsteps sounded on the first flight of stairs, then faded. Silence fell over the flat, lingered, and was broken by the sound of a car engine from the narrow street. That died away into the night, and only silence was left.

.   .   .   .   .

They had been gone for at least a quarter of an hour. Martin was on his knees ; they were agonising. He hardly knew how he had managed to turn and then kneel on the bare boards, for there were only rugs on the floor. He was several feet away from the telephone, and moved towards it,

dragging his knees. Richard was behind him. He wasn't
sure what he would be able to do when he reached the
telephone; the first task was to get to it.

He reached the shelf on which it stood, close to the fire-
place. He couldn't see it. It was a low shelf; kneeling, he
could press his chest against it. He did so, heavily, and tried
to get to his feet, using his chest as a lever; it wouldn't
work. The bare boards tortured his knees. He turned
round slowly, then leaned back against the shelf; he could
touch it with his bound hands. He pressed heavily, straining
every muscle, and was suddenly on one knee. After that it
was easy to stand, but directly he stood upright his head
reeled and he fell against the shelves. The telephone gave a
slight ringing sound as it moved. He stood for a few seconds,
steadying, then turned with his back to the telephone. His
fingers were cramped and he felt pins and needles stabbing
through them, but he could touch the telephone dial-piece.

He knocked the receiver off; it dropped to the shelf, but
didn't fall farther.

He could dial 999; that would call the police, and when
they heard no answer, they would almost certainly trace the
address, and come here. They would probably be here in a
few minutes, but—would that help? Because it was easy to
dial without being able to see the telephone, the temptation
was great. Richard's plight added to it. He put a finger in
the hole, started to twist the dial, then took his finger away
and the dial whirred back.

He could call Barbara. She lived near. Temple Bar
88511. TEM 88511. He had dialled the number hundreds
of times, but always when looking at the dial. Could he do
it, blindly, back to the instrument? He concentrated, trying
to remember the letters of each dial hole. Then he started.
T—if he were lucky. E—he was sure of E. M—he hoped
it was M.

Fool! If he dialled o, he would get the operator, she
would put him through. He managed to reach above the
dial and tap down the bar to break the connection, then
dialled o. There was an immediate answer. He gave the
number, but he was so far from the mouthpiece that he had
to say it twice before the operator repeated it. The same
happened when he gave his own number.

" Hold on, please," said the operator.

He turned and bent down farther, moving his chin until he touched the receiver ; moved until he could feel the mouthpiece. His back threatened to break in two. The ringing tone went on. Was it late ? No, it wasn't much after ten, Barbara wouldn't be asleep. She might be out, but she hadn't said she would be, she would normally have been expecting a call for the last hour. Anyhow, she was convalescing, she wouldn't go out.

On and on, on and on . . .

" Hallo ? " It was a woman's voice, and he thought it sounded breathless. His ear was close to the earpiece, which meant that his lips were some way from the mouthpiece. He shouted.

" Barbara ! "

" Hallo, who——— " He couldn't be sure that it was Barbara's voice, until she exclaimed, " Scoop ! "

" Hurry round here. Hurry. The flat. Bring your key." He shouted the terse sentences, knew that he was alarming her, but couldn't keep his voice low.

He heard her say, " Five minutes," and ring off. He could straighten up again. He leaned against the shelves, with the top one cutting into his thigh painfully, but the relief to his back was so great that the lesser pain didn't matter.

After a while he moved slowly across the room towards Richard. He couldn't see his brother, there was only darkness.

.   .   .   .   .

He heard the taxi stop, and then drive off.

He heard Barbara coming up the stairs. He would never mistake her footsteps.

Her key scraped against the lock, but it seemed an age before the door opened.

" Scoop ! " The darkness hit her frighteningly. " Scoop, are you——— "

" All right," he said quietly. " Just put the light on. Richard's been knocked out."

He closed his eyes against the light, and marvelled that he could say, " Richard's been knocked out." He saw Barbara, as he opened his eyes. She was tall, dark, and lovely, with a freshness which always surprised him, no matter when he saw her. She wore a green tweed suit beneath a fur coat— no hat, no gloves. Fear filled her eyes when she saw him standing still, then she looked at Richard.

The patches were red; blood. Richard looked as pale as the dawn.

" Never mind me," said Martin gruffly. " Look at him."

5   MORNING

BARBARA stood with her finger on Richard's pulse, looking down at him. Martin didn't feel quite so bad; Richard was breathing, and seemed to be breathing easily. Barbara let his wrist go, turned, and smiled; and the smile caught at Martin's heart; it always did.

" Near enough to normal," she said. " I'll cut you free." She hurried to the kitchen, without making a fuss, came back with a small vegetable-knife, and cut through the cord at his wrist. He let his hands fall to his sides; the pain of circulating blood was so great that he bit his lips against it. Barbara pulled up a chair and held his shoulders as he sat down. Then she took off her coat and covered Richard with it, to keep him warm, next turned, went down on her knees, and began to massage Martin's wrists. Her hands were long and slim, she had no varnish on the nails. She had no make-up on, either, yet her complexion was superb. Her eyes were huge as she looked up at him, head back, hair falling away from her broad forehead.

He bent his head and kissed her hair.

" I'm all right. See to Richard," he said.

" In a minute." She was fond of Richard, but was one of the few who was always prepared to believe that Richard usually got whatever he deserved; she was almost proof against his charm. She massaged for several minutes, until Martin's wrists and hands were tingling but no longer pain-ful. Then she turned to Richard again. She knew a bit about first aid, and the fact that she wasn't alarmed for him convinced Martin that the wound wasn't really serious. She moved the hair aside, frowned, prodded a little where the hair was matted with blood, then touched the rest of his head. She nodded.

" That's only a scratch," she said. " The blood, I mean. He had a bang over the head which knocked him out, he shouldn't be unconscious for long." She moved away. " I'll get blankets and a hot-water bottle."

She was gone for ten minutes; Martin could hear her moving about the kitchen. He chose that moment for calling himself a fool, because they weren't married, and he wasn't sharing the flat with her, instead of with Richard. Put it down to pride. He wanted to make a success of Prince Agency before he married Barbara, who worked in it; it was hard to imagine the agency without her.

She came back, as Richard stirred, muttered, and fell silent again.

" He'll soon be round." Barbara put the hot-water bottle at his feet, took off the coat, and covered him with blankets, then went back for water and a towel. Richard's eyes were opening, and he looked about him dully as she sponged the wound; Martin soon saw for himself that it wasn't serious.

Richard muttered, " What's going on ? " He scowled. " Where are the bad men ? "

" Martin drove them away," said Barbara promptly. " You keep quiet for a bit." She pulled up a chair, sat down, and held out her hand for a cigarette. Martin, feeling almost himself again, lit it for her and waited for her to ask :

" Well, what's it all about ? "

He told her, with Richard lying on his back and looking at him, and Barbara's eyes showing swift changes of emotion as the story unfolded.

.   .   .   .   .

They talked for some time. Richard, obviously much better, hitched himself up on the cushions and joined in, careful to make sure that his comments were worth consideration. Nothing profound came out of the conference, but gradually an issue arose : to tell the police or not. This case was serious. The men who had lain in wait might be killers; probably were. There seemed no doubt of Rhoda Grenfell's fear for her mother, and sooner or later the police would probably hear about it. They would not take kindly to discovering that the Fane brothers had been working on the case for some time; it might disturb a relationship with Scotland Yard which, if it wasn't exactly brotherly, was at least cordial. Barbara and Martin raised the issue, without facing it. Richard, smoking his third cigarette in half an hour, blew smoke rings towards the celling, and said:

" It would be crazy to tell the Yard yet."

The others simply looked at him.

" I know, I know," said Richard. " I've crashed my big feet in where angels would fear to tread. I still say that it would be crazy to tell the Yard. Once they get their hands on it, we'll be out. Once we're out, we lose our fee. Did it ever occur to either of you that we're in this for money ? "

" Hush," said Barbara. " You oughtn't to mention the word."

" I've earned as much for Prince as either of you," said Richard, not without truth.

" And taken twice as much out," said Martin pithily. " You might pause to think what's the right thing to do, apart from how we'll get the most money."

Richard looked faintly disgusted.

" I can hear the Maestro talking, but the difference between you and our revered father is that he's comfortably off and we're next door to being paupers. He can afford to sit back and talk about right and wrong, you've got to earn your living."

" *Our* living," Barbara said.

" I know what's the matter with you two lovebirds," said Richard scathingly. " As soon as we've four figures to our credit, you'll shoot off and get married and leave me to hold the fort while you're honeymooning. It wouldn't be a bad idea if you fixed it by special licence right away. When I'm working on my own, the profits will start going up. Until then, we shan't have a chance."

" When you're in charge, we'll be put out of business. You'll cock a snook at the Yard, and they'll close us up," said Martin without vehemence.

Richard shrugged.

" Sheer envy, but I forgive you." He turned over on his side, winced a little, but soon went on, " The trouble with you two, as well as with the Maestro, is that you get all worked up about right and wrong and forget that our job is to do right by the client. Who's most likely to get results ? The Yard, or us ? This is a family business, everyone is keeping plenty up their sleeve, if you see what I mean. Put the Yard on to it, and the Grenfells will close up like clams. You did a neat job at the flat, Scoop," Richard added disarmingly. " There were times when I thought you were mishandling it, but no—Rhoda will come in the morning and tell you the truth. When you have it you can decide if it's a police job or not. Before you make it a police job, you'll have to tell Grenfell. No sense in ringing the Yard to-night, anyhow. You say the chap who pulled a gun on us here said dark things would happen *if* you listened to Rhoda. So they won't happen until you've had a chance to listen. You can sleep easy."

Martin considered.

" Something in that," he conceded. " Agree, Bar ? "

" I think so."

" It takes the pair of you to reach a decision when it's staring you in the face," said Richard. " Tell you what, Bar, I could do with a cup of tea. Think you've the strength to make one ? "

Martin grinned. " He gets things right occasionally. I'll help you."

" No conspiring behind my back," warned Richard.

In the kitchen, waiting for the kettle to boil, Barbara yawned as she said :

" One thing's certain—*ooooh, dear !*—you mustn't let this Grenfell girl come here or go to the office in the morning. If you're going to see her, you'll have to do it secretly. She might be followed wherever she goes, too."

Martin, smoking his pipe again, nodded.

" So it won't be easy."

Martin shook his head.

" I can try to find out what there is to know about her and this Hilda Kennedy," Barbara went on, " but the thing to make sure of is that the men who came here to-night don't know that we're working on it. Not yet, anyhow. It might be a good idea if I were to see Rhoda Grenfell. I could arrange to meet her at a tea-shop in the morning—that's if she decides to talk. We could 'phone her about that. I probably won't be recognised by any one who's watching her."

"You probably would be," Martin said dryly. "No, I'll see her. We can fix a secret meeting. I'll ring her early in the morning. Bad move, really, I'd rather she came without prompting, but it can't be helped. When I've seen her, you can have a go—you'll see through her, if she's been lying. It'll take time." He spoke slowly, turning everything over in his mind several times; he deceived most people into thinking that he was a slow thinker. "Is Richard all right, or ought he to see a doctor?"

"If he'd stay in bed to-morrow he'd almost forget that he'd been hit," said Barbara. Her eyes brightened. "It might be a good idea to have a doctor, though—Neil would come like a shot, and would tell him he must stay in bed for a day or two. He couldn't get up to anything if he were here. We might even get him to go down to Nairn Lodge." Her eyes lit up. "He'd probably jump at the chance, he'd beg some money from Mother, and come back feeling on top of the world."

"Do we want him on top of the world?" murmured Martin.

Barbara, pouring water into the tea-pot, grimaced.

"I see what you mean. In any case, he'll be so anxious to make amends for what happened to-night that he'll probably take wild chances. Try to get him down to Dorset——"

"Barbara," said Richard from the door, "I'm disappointed in you. In both of you." His voice was sepulchral, he had some colour, although his eyes were rather too bright. "You might as well try to get to the moon as try to send me down to Dorset while you stay here and risk your necks. It takes you half an hour to make a cup of tea!" He scowled. "We're in this together. Don't forget it."

"Go and lie down," Barbara said sharply. "If you play the fool, you'll really be ill."

"And how you'd love that," said Richard bitterly. He shrugged, and went back to the big room.

He was subdued when Barbara left, a little before midnight, and had little to say to Martin as they went to bed. Martin felt uneasy; it never helped when Richard thought that he was having a poor deal.

He put his head round the door of Richard's small room.

" How's the head ? "

" A lot clearer than yours is ever likely to be," said Richard sourly.

" Good! Good night."

" 'Night," growled Richard.

Martin went to bed, but didn't get off to sleep at once. Richard wasn't acting in character. Usually he would be heavily reproachful, but it was unlike him to show or feel bitterness at what he had overheard. The blow over the head might have been more serious than they thought; if he were really feeling ill, it would explain his mood. He might have a guilty conscience, too; but nothing in the night's events would explain Richard feeling guilty for as long as this. He seldom minded being made to look a fool, after the first wound to his vanity was over.

Martin could see more in Richard's favour now than he had for some days. Richard's careless extravagance with money had got under his skin, and biased him.

They'd probably both feel better in the morning.

. . . . .

It was still dark when Martin woke. He lay for a few minutes, looking at the faint outline of the window, and then put an arm out of the warm bedclothes, felt the bite of the cold morning air, turned the small bedside clock, and saw from the illuminated face that it was five minutes past seven. He needn't call Rhoda Grenfell before half-past eight, so there was no great hurry. He lay snug and warm. There was no sound from the other bedroom. If Richard had slept well, he would be feeling much better.

Martin got up at a quarter to eight, tied a woollen dressing-gown about him tightly, shivered, and went out. He didn't look into Richard's room, but went to the kitchen and put on the kettle. He turned back towards the bedrooms, and was half-way up the stairs before the telephone began to ring. It sounded very loud. It would probably wake Richard, when another hour's sleep would do him a lot of good.

Martin swore mildly as he hurried into the big room, snatched up the telephone, and barked:

" Hallo ? "

" Just a reminder," a man said. " Drop this Rhoda Grenfell job, or you'll get hurt."

The voice was vaguely familiar: the gunman's. There was a pause before he hung up.

Martin put down his receiver slowly. He went across to the windows, drew the curtains, looked into the street, and saw several trucks and vans coming away from Covent Garden, loaded with fruit and vegetables; mostly vegetables. He went to Richard's door, listened outside, heard nothing, and went to the kitchen; the kettle was boiling furiously, water was spitting over the floor. He made tea for one, put the kettle on a low gas, and sat on a corner of the kitchen table, smoking a cigarette and sipping the hot, weak tea.

Scotland Yard might be able to help trace Claude. Was there a way of getting help from the Yard without explaining fully? Richard would jeer at him for posing the question; it would be easy. It was something to do quickly. He'd better bath and shave, there was no reason why he shouldn't call Rhoda Grenfell before half-past eight; the fact that she would guess that he was anxious to know more would have to be risked. He finished his second cup of tea and went to the bathroom.

The telephone bell rang again.

He turned the taps off, and hurried into the big room. The ringing still sounded very loud. He took off the receiver. It wouldn't surprise him to know that this was the man again, working on his nerves.

" Hallo ? "

" Martin Fane ? " It was a crisp voice; Grenfell's.

" Yes. Good morning."

Grenfell said, " Fane, there's been an ugly development. I want a word with you before you see the police. When can I see you ? "

Martin said heavily, " Whenever you like. What's happened ? "

Grenfell said very deliberately, " My sister-in-law has been murdered."

.   .   .   .   .

Martin shaved quickly and washed hurriedly; Grenfell was coming here, and would probably arrive at any minute now. He'd given no details, but he'd meant what he said, the case had taken the ugliest possible turn. Grenfell seemed to take it for granted that Martin would have to go to the police now; for a reason he couldn't properly understand, Martin liked that idea less than he had the night before. He didn't forget that Rhoda Grenfell had said that her mother and her uncle had quarrelled; and Grenfell had admitted that they were on bad terms.

Martin went into the big room, still in his dressing-gown, to telephone Barbara, changed his mind, and decided to see Richard first. If Richard were awake, he'd better be told what had happened. He heard a car pull up outside; it was almost certainly Grenfell. He opened Richard's door; if Richard woke up on hearing voices he would probably break in at a bad moment. If he were sound asleep, Grenfell could be warned to keep his voice low.

He peered into the room.

Richard wasn't there.

6 TALE OF MURDER

MARTIN stood with his hand on the door, gripping it tightly. He oughtn't to be surprised; now that he knew Richard had gone, his brother's mood of the previous night was fully explained. Richard was determined to re-establish himself. He had known that going off alone was a crazy thing to do, but had been set on it. Anyone who knew him well ought to have guessed his likely move; if he'd had any sense, Martin would have put a padlock on the door. Richard hadn't been badly hurt, but would be short of the little bit of zest needed for whatever escapade he had launched.

Martin's grip on the door relaxed. He went into the big room as the front-door bell rang. He called, "Just a minute!" as he reached the telephone, and dialled Barbara's number; she answered promptly.

"Can't stay, sweet. Richard's gone lone-wolfing. Rhoda's

mother was murdered last night. Don't do anything yet— don't leave your flat. Grenfell's just come to talk to me."

He gave her no chance to answer, but rang off; at least he could rely on Barbara's good sense. Grenfell must have heard him, for he hadn't pressed the bell again. Martin reached the front door, pulled the bolt, and opened the door.

Grenfell looked pale and ill.

" I'm all right," he muttered. " Banged my head on the door of the car. Hell of a bump."

Martin had to help him up the steps and into the big room. Grenfell's eyes were closed, and Martin made him more comfortable, with a pillow at his head.

" Thanks. Given me a wicked headache."

" I'll get some aspirins." Martin fetched them from the first-aid box in the bathroom, then made a cup of tea. As Grenfell sipped it Martin studied him; the man looked much older than he had on the previous night.

" I'll be all right."

" Take it easy for a few minutes," advised Martin. He went out, to avoid tempting Grenfell to talk, and left the man alone for fully ten minutes. When he went back, Grenfell's eyes were clearer and he looked much better.

" Easier ? " Martin asked. Silly question.

Grenfell said, " Much, but I've still a shocking headache. What did I tell you over the telephone ? "

" A tale of murder," Martin said. " No details at all."

" Have the police telephoned you yet ? " asked Grenfell.

" Why should they ? " Martin asked. He was reminding himself that this man and the murdered woman had quarrelled a lot.

" Rhoda's bound to tell them that they wanted you to help," said Grenfell.

Martin nodded. He wasn't sure that the other was right, but that didn't greatly matter. He wasn't going to prompt Grenfell at this stage; he would just sit back and listen to what the man told him. Grenfell would say exactly what he wanted to say, and no more. He knew that there was a danger that he wouldn't be able to guard his tongue properly; so he would probably say less than he had intended to.

Grenfell sat up more erect, and took a cigarette. Martin stood against the table, watching.

" I've never liked it," Grenfell said. " The way my
sister-in-law and her daughter have behaved, I mean. I was
afraid they would run into serious trouble. There isn't
much I can do. In my position——" He broke off,
looked earnest, almost appealing; as if pleading with
Martin to understand what he was driving at. Martin remained obtuse. " Easily shot at," Grenfell went on.
" Can't use a newspaper to screen myself or my family
against scandal—against police investigation. I was nervous
in case the police stepped in. That's partly why I didn't use
one of the *Clarion's* men," he added abruptly.

" What's the other reason ? " Martin asked.

" Hilda Kennedy knows most of them," Grenfell said,
and hesitated. Then he gave a little, secretive smile, and
went on briskly. " A private inquiry agency has a lot of
scope—lot of rope, too. I know you have to be careful, but
the police don't expect you to tell them everything you know.
Do they ? "

" They might take it hard if I don't."

" Only if it's material fact which they could use," Grenfell
said dryly. " And you're on good terms with them. You
could work on this case without treading on any corns. Last
night I asked you to find out what was troubling Rhoda ;
now I want you to investigate the murder of my sister-in-law
as well, and do it without any more contact with the police
than is absolutely necessary. *I* want the information. If
I can, I want to help Rhoda."

Martin said heavily, " I see." He fancied that Grenfell
looked surprised ; perhaps disappointed. Grenfell had
expected someone much more lively ; Richard, for instance.
That set Martin wondering where Richard was, and how he
was faring ; he wrenched his thoughts back to the immediate
problem. " Trouble is, Grenfell, that no one who's
approached me in this case likes telling me everything. I
can't do anything with less. Take you, for instance." He
smiled faintly, and Grenfell looked as if he preferred this to
apparent dullness. " You think Rhoda might have killed
her mother, don't you ? "

Grenfell didn't answer.

" Rhoda came to me with a story and a lot of reservations,
but she was in trouble, all right. I could blame myself for

sending her away, I could even think that if I'd listened more, I might have saved her mother. But you're asking yourself whether Rhoda did it, after coming and telling me a story intended to prove that a third party was after her. Aren't you ? "

Grenfell said, " It could be."

" Didn't mother and daughter get along ? "

" I don't think they were—the best of friends." Grenfell hesitated. " Not lately. Not since Rhoda came under the influence of Hilda Kennedy."

Martin thought, " Where does he want to take me ? " and waited. Grenfell meant him to regard Hilda Kennedy as a lively suspect, if nothing else.

" Bad influence," Grenfell went on abruptly. " You've heard of Hilda Kennedy, of course."

" No."

" You don't read the right newspapers," said Grenfell. " I gave you a pretty broad hint when I told you that many of my reporters know her. She's been featured in the *Sunday Clarion* for a long time. She runs our astrology feature. *Your* FATE *in the Stars*." He emphasised the word " fate ". " In some ways she's brilliantly clever. Each month she makes forecasts of national and world events, and often gets surprisingly near the truth. Guesswork, of course, but—— " He shrugged. " She's a very big following."

" I see," said Martin dryly. " And helps the *Sunday Clarion's* circulation."

" Quite a bit," Grenfell admitted. " Rhoda followed her horoscopes in the *Clarion* and was convinced that Hilda Kennedy was gifted with second sight. Strangely enough, her mother didn't fall for that. Martha wasn't brilliant, but she had no faith in fortune-tellers or astrologers. I think that she fell out with Rhoda because of Hilda Kennedy. Mind you, I don't know. I wish I did. I'm telling you everything I know, Fane, even if I didn't tell you everything I feared."

Martin said, " Everything helps. What are you really asking me to do ? Investigate the life of Hilda Kennedy ? "

" It would be worth trying," said Grenfell. " Especially the degree of her influence over Rhoda—and the reason for it. Not that I think you've far to look for the reason. Rhoda has too much money, and rogues of both sexes are continually trying to relieve her of some of it. As for what I want you to do first—I've told you. Find out who killed Rhoda's mother—and find out all you can about Hilda Kennedy."

"Fee?" asked Martin.

Grenfell laughed. "Double what we agreed last night. A thousand pounds bonus, if you get results before the police. That's fair enough, isn't it?"

Martin said abruptly, "I'll have a shot at it. How did you learn about the murder?"

"A servant of my sister-in-law told me by telephone—I told her to call the police, and not to tell them she had telephoned me until after they arrived. I wanted time to arrange this with you. If you're wondering whether there's any chance that she's wrong and it wasn't murder—I don't think so. Martha was stabbed, through the breast, to the heart. That's as much as I can tell you."

"It's enough." Martin spoke without enthusiasm—he might have shown some, but he thought suddenly of Richard, and where Richard might be. "Are you feeling well enough to drive?"

Grenfell was getting up.

"Oh, I'm all right." Grenfell went slowly towards the door. "My head's not as steady as I like, I hope I haven't talked too much." He smiled, much more himself. "I know you'll do everything you can, Fane." He held out his hand.

Martin took it, watched him start down the stairs, then went to the window which overlooked the street. Grenfell soon appeared, and walked to his car as if he were perfectly normal. He glanced up and down the road before taking the wheel, and drove off too fast. Martin watched closely; no one appeared to take any interest in the newspaper magnate, and certainly the car wasn't followed.

Grenfell might be trying to lay a false trail; might be the killer. Was that in character with a man of his position and calibre? Martin didn't try to guess, not knowing the man well enough yet.

He ought to go to Mrs. Sydney Grenfell's flat; the police wouldn't give him much scope, but he might pick up something. He ought to try to see Rhoda, and Hilda Kennedy would be worth attention.

He went to Richard's room, as if to convince himself that it was really empty.

The bedclothes were rumpled; Richard had been restless. The suit he had worn the day before was on a hanger outside a small wardrobe. Martin rummaged in the wardrobe; an old suit was missing, a suit Richard wore whenever he wanted to give the impression of being down-and-out; he called it his working-suit. Most of the crazy things he had done had been while wearing that. Martin scowled, and went across to the dressing-table. One drawer was usually locked; it wasn't now. Martin felt his heart thumping. There should be an automatic pistol inside.

Martin pulled the drawer open.

The gun was gone.

So Richard had dressed for " work " and taken the gun, which meant that he had gone looking for trouble, following some idea which he'd nursed the night before while smarting to justify himself. The after-effects of the blow over the head probably made him only half-effective. If he caught up with trouble, he might have a lot of difficulty getting out of it.

" The crazy fool," Martin said aloud—and then jumped, for the telephone bell rang. He swung towards it; this might be Richard.

" Hallo ? "

" Mr. Fane ? Mr. Martin Fane ? " It was Rhoda Grenfell, speaking so excitedly that her words ran into one another.

" Yes."

" I must see you," Rhoda said urgently. " Please stay there until—— "

" Hold on ! " Martin said sharply. " Listen to me."

7

MEETING-PLACE

Rhoda didn't hang up, but waited. Martin formed his words carefully, she sounded in a mood when she would listen impatiently; he didn't want silly mistakes.

"I'll see you, but not here. You mustn't come here or go to the office. Do you understand?"

"Yes, but——"

"Listen. Have you a pencil?"

"I—wait a minute." The receiver clattered, and she was gone for half a minute; she sounded breathless when she came back. "Yes, I've a pencil and paper."

"Go to Glanville House, Arundel Street," said Martin slowly. "That's off the Strand, opposite the far end of Aldwych. Go to the office of Matthew Matten, the literary agent."

"The what?"

"Literary agent. Matthew Matten, M–A–T–T–E–N. It's on the top floor. Be there at half-past nine—not sooner, for no one will be in. And wait for me. Have you got all that?"

She repeated the name and address, and went on with a rush, "But can't I go straight away? It's urgent, you can't have heard about my mother."

"I've heard. I'm—sorry."

"It's terrible. And the police will want to ask me a lot of questions, I wanted to see you before they could."

"Where are you?"

"At Hilda Kennedy's place, but——"

"If you think the police might find you there, go out," said Martin. "Have some tea or coffee somewhere. You haven't much time to wait." He hesitated, and she muttered something which sounded like "All right". He said good-bye and rang off. He put the receiver down slowly, and stood by the telephone.

The Grenfell family was anxious to see him before the police could question them, and he wasn't sure that he liked the way they acted.

It was twenty minutes to nine. There wasn't time to try to get into the murdered woman's flat, and in any case he ought to see Rhoda first. He rang a newspaper man he knew well, and everything that Grenfell had told him was confirmed; there was nothing new.

He went into the kitchen and ate some cornflakes and a boiled egg; breakfast took ten minutes. His ears were cocked for the telephone, but it didn't ring. He dressed quickly and was ready for the street at nine-fifteen. He went to his wardrobe, where he kept his automatic, hesitated, decided not to take it with him, and went to the front door; he paused there for a few seconds, hoping that the bell would ring, bringing news of Richard. Every good quality in Richard sprang to mind now.

He went out, slamming the door. At the foot of the stairs he listened again; there wasn't a sound. He turned along the street towards the parking plot; the white Buick was gone. He hadn't expected to find it. He walked towards the Strand, glancing behind him at the corners; he wasn't followed. He turned left towards Arundel Street—his office was in the other direction. In the Strand everyone was hustling; it was too early for shop-window dawdlers. The sun was up, the sky was clear; the frost on the roofs and, here and there, on the pavement and road, was rapidly melting. Satisfied that he wasn't followed, he reached Glanville House.

Matten was his father's agent and a reliable ally. He was an elderly, rather vague man to those who did not know him, and he could be relied upon to be at the office by half-past nine; so could his staff. The old-fashioned building was gloomy, and the antiquated lift wasn't at the ground floor. Martin waited, and several people joined him. Two had to wait for the lift's return.

The passage outside Matten's office was empty, but he hadn't reached the door before he heard Rhoda's voice:

" I'm sure he said he would be here by half-past nine. I must—— " She opened the door and put her head out, and her face cleared. In this poor light she seemed better-looking than she had the night before. The murder of her mother hadn't affected her appearance much. She wore a heavy tweed coat with big sleeves, and a hat of the same warm brown material. " Oh, there you are ! "

" 'Morning," said Martin, and went inside. There were two small offices between this and Matten's own office; all the doors were open. Grey-haired, mild-mannered Matten was in the doorway of his room. " Hallo, Matthew," Martin said. " Can I be a hound, and use your office for ten minutes or so ? "

" Of course." Matten blinked. " Give me two

minutes." He smiled vaguely at Rhoda Grenfell. " If the young lady will wait." He took Martin's arm, drew him inside, and closed the door firmly on Rhoda's impatient gasp.

Nothing ever hurried Matten. He claimed that no man who served as go-between with authors, editors, and publishers could survive unless he had the patience of Job. He had wispy hair and a bald patch, and dressed in a black coat and striped trousers. He kept hold of Martin's arm, tightly. In an outer office a girl started to type.

Matten looked up at Martin.

"What's young Richard up to ? " he asked.

Martin said sharply, " Heard from him ? "

" Yes. He's excited, and I think he's nervous. You're to go to this address as soon as you can, and you're not to do anything else until you've seen him." Matten's faded eyes twinkled. " He was very insistent. He rang you, but you were out, and he asked me to find you—I'd just rung your office when the young woman came, and told me you would soon be here." Matten put a slip of paper into Martin's hand. " Now you'd better see that imperious young woman." He patted Martin's arm, and went to the door, while Martin glanced down at the slip of paper. The address was 15 The Grove, Fulham, and meant nothing to Martin.

The door burst open.

" Why on earth have you kept me waiting like this ? " demanded Rhoda Grenfell; it wouldn't take much to make her angry—or tearful.

Martin said, " Sorry."

" It's dreadful! I knew she was in danger, she wouldn't tell me what it was about, but I knew she was. Now I—— " She broke off.

" You're frightened."

She said slowly and deliberately, " I'm *terrified*."

" Thinking it might happen to you ? "

" It could," said the girl. " I just don't understand it, but—I want you to find the murderer. I don't trust the police—— "

" That's nonsense," said Martin calmly.

She didn't flare up, but moved away and sat on the edge

of a large desk which was placed slantwise in the small office. The walls were lined with books ; one wall was reserved for the voluminous output of Martin's father, and on the spines of many of the jackets was the word " Prince " with a crown on top.

Rhoda said slowly, " It isn't nonsense, but I know what you mean. I want you to find out who killed Mother, and why—and I want you to find out before the police do. Please." She sounded very young.

" What time did it happen ? Do you know ? "

" No, I just didn't hear a thing. I know nothing—nothing ! " Her voice rose. " At least you could try to help."

" Yes," said Martin. " I'll try—on one condition."

She stood upright, suddenly eager.

" I'll agree to anything ! "

" Good. Sit down, take your time, and tell me exactly what's happening, why you and Miss Kennedy played that trick on Richard last night, and everything you know. Tell me everything you ought to tell the police but don't want to."

She didn't sit down, but said evenly, " Last night you said you had to be judge of what you passed on to the police. Does that still stand ? "

" Of course." Martin, solemn-faced until then, smiled. At certain moments he caught all the charm that Richard had and, because it was unexpected, it could be devastating. He leaned forward and held the girl's arm. " I have to make that reservation, but I'd only tell the police if it seemed essential to help them catch a crook. Prince hasn't built up a reputation by squealing to the police. Read his books ? "

" Most of them," she said, and looked relieved. " I *must* tell someone."

" Come and sit down." Martin moved a chair.

" I'd rather walk about," said Rhoda. " It may seem silly to you. Part of it, anyhow. Mother and I quarrelled, because I'm so friendly with Hilda Kennedy. They're old—acquaintances." She used that word deliberately, eschewing " friend ". " I think Hilda has remarkable gifts, and Mother talked a lot of nonsense, about her wanting to influence me because of money." The girl shrugged, as if the idea was absurd. " That's why I'm not so close to my mother—— "

She stopped abruptly, and turned and looked out of the window, with a view of the Thames through the house-tops. She stood quite still, back to Martin, as she went on:

" That's why I *wasn't* so close to her. We shared the flat, of course."

" Where is the flat ? "

" Fifteen Mowbray Crescent, St. John's Wood. The police are there now, of course. It's—dreadful! I—I wasn't in very much. A few days ago—Saturday, I think it was—she came into my bedroom. She said she was frightened, wouldn't explain why, just said she couldn't bear being alone so much. I thought it was a kind of trick, to keep me at home more, and didn't take much notice. ˙When I got home that night, she was walking about the flat, like a woman demented. She still wouldn't explain, but talked about danger and being afraid all the time. She'd seen Uncle Edward—that's Sir Edward Grenfell—and he'd been in a bad mood, they'd quarrelled again." She didn't dwell on Grenfell's part, seemed to drop it in quite naturally. " I realised she was serious about her fears, but—I hate saying this about her now, but I have to—she's always been rather neurotic. Well, I calmed her down. Next day she was rather better, but the day after she was just as bad.

" I could have talked to my uncle, but—well, he's been so unfriendly, and he'd have said it was neurotic nonsense. I talked to Hilda about it. You know she's an astrologer, don't you ? She said she'd seen danger in mother's horoscope, and agreed that we had to do something about it. Then mother got a wild idea that she wouldn't leave the flat, said she daren't go out. She didn't go outside for several days. I was so worried I had to see someone, and—I chose you. I read about you in a newspaper somewhere."

Martin was solemn; the occasion demanded that.

" So I tried," Rhoda went on. " You know what happened. Oh, there's this : Hilda's very matter of fact in some things, and suggested Mother should go to the police. Mother nearly had a fit when I said so, she hated the idea so much. That's why I was emphatic."

Martin mused; " I see. And you can't tell me anything more about it."

" Not a thing."

" Does anyone else know that there's been trouble ? "

" Not as far as I know," said Rhoda, and then added carelessly, " Except my uncle. He was at the flat yesterday morning and again last night. Mother's never really liked him, she wouldn't say anything to him and flatly denied that there was anything the matter. She was very strong in her likes and dislikes. Her dislikes became almost hatred."

" When did the trouble start ? "

" Looking back, I think it's been going on for some time. Months. In fact, *almost* since my father died. Sometimes I've wondered if it could be *money*." Rhoda spoke as if it were an outrageous possibility. " She hated it when Uncle Edward had some control over the estate—he did, for a while. But I don't think it can be money, she had oodles."

" Oodles, eh ? " Martin changed his tone abruptly. " Now tell me why you held up my brother with a gun and called me to bail him out."

She changed colour, and seemed to lose her self-confidence.

" That was a mistake," she said. " I mean, I didn't—— "

" You mean it wasn't your idea, don't you ? Hilda took charge, and you just did what she told you, because—— "

" That's unfair ! " exclaimed Rhoda. " Hilda doesn't take charge of me."

" You're sure she hasn't some hold—— "

" No ! It's a lie, I don't care who told you. They all say Hilda has a hold over me, and—— "

" They ? "

" Oh, everyone." She was breathing hard. " Please believe me, Hilda is just a good friend. I was just as responsible as she was last night—it was just that we felt a bit scared at having a—a burglar." Her voice softened again. " Will you help me ? "

He paused to consider.

" If I can—and if you're frank," he said.

Rhoda fumbled with her bag.

" I don't mind what it costs, I—— "

" Let's worry about money afterwards. I may not earn any. And I won't cheat you." Martin smiled again. " There's absolutely nothing you've told me that you need keep away from the police. Tell them. They're good at finding out when witnesses are keeping anything back. Tell them everything."

"Even about you?"

"Oh, yes."

"I suppose you know what you're talking about," said Rhoda Grenfell. She began to draw on her gloves; all her movements were graceful.

"I do, in this," said Martin. "There's one thing you haven't told me, by the way."

"What's that?" Her voice was sharp.

"How did you come round to thinking that you might be in danger yourself?"

Rhoda said slowly, "It's so hard to explain. Mother said several times that she wasn't only frightened for herself, but for me as well. Oh, I did forget! She said that she was worried because I was away from the flat so much, she couldn't feel sure that I was safe. When you have that kind of talk thrown at you a few times, you begin to wonder. And now this dreadful thing has happened——"

She broke off, swung towards the window, and stood without moving for at least two minutes. When she turned, her eyes were shining, as if with tears. Martin didn't say much more, but took her out and to the lift. She didn't want him to go down with her, but he insisted. They shook hands at the lift gate, and she went out into the street. He followed for a few yards, but kept in the entrance hall of the building, watching her; Richard would have called that a hunch.

Rhoda was nearly out of sight when Martin saw the man. He was tall, good-looking in a sallow way. His face lit up at sight of Rhoda, and they went off together. Martin watched them as far as the end of the street, and turned back to the lift.

Why had she told the young man where she was? Why hadn't she mentioned him? How much of her story was true?

Martin started to ring for the lift, and then realised that he needn't go upstairs again. He wanted to get to the dead woman's flat, but he had another, more urgent job; to see Richard. But for Richard's head wound, he would have taken a chance and gone to St. John's Wood first. Getting Richard out of trouble wouldn't help much towards solving a murder mystery.   He took a taxi to a garage near the flat, hired a car, and drove through the West End towards Fulham and the south-west suburbs.   Now that he had freed his mind for thinking about Richard, he didn't like the way Richard had sent that message.   Richard was in a jam.

He didn't like the look of The Grove, either.   It was a street of mean, narrow houses, in a poor part of Fulham. The street seemed to be all eyes; he felt that every movement he made was watched and noted, as he drove along slowly, looking for Number 15.

8   RICHARD

MARTIN slowed down near the end of the street, stopping just beyond Number 15.   That house seemed no different from all the others—two-storeyed, narrow, grey, with the paintwork in bad condition.   The lace curtains at the windows were so bright a cream that they looked yellow. Two spiky leaves of an aspidistra touched the glass; a sign, at one time, of respectability.   Every house had that look of lower-middle-class respectability which had fallen on bad days.

The door opened.

" Hallo, old chap," said Richard.

He wore the old suit, he hadn't shaved, his right eye was bloodshot, and yet he retained the attractiveness.   It was in his smile, in spite of its sheepishness, and in his eyes.

" Come in."

He waited until Martin had entered, then led the way into the front room.   This was small, crowded with furniture and had a smell of polish.   The walls were thick with large and small photographs and prints and a silk shade with long tassels hung from the single lamp, in the middle of the ceiling.   The windows were closed; as if the sun were an enemy here.

" Like a cup of tea ? "   Richard was nervous, and hiding it with brightness. Martin hesitated.   They had sharp differences, but nothing had destroyed, or even greatly affected, lifelong trust and liking. He probably knew Richard better than Richard knew him; he had the observant mind, and forgot little. If he handled this wrongly, Richard might take it hard. The offer of tea was an olive branch.

He grinned. " If you can work the miracle."

" Two shakes of a lamb's tail," said Richard, and hurried out of the room. Martin heard him talking. He was soon back, smiling, looking more relaxed; the gloom of the room hid his bloodshot eye. " Glad you made it pretty fast, Scoop. This is one time when I need a big brother."

" Oh, we have our uses. Next time you shoot off, leave a farewell note, will you? I'd hate to lose you without a last fond word."

Richard grinned. " Solved everything?" he demanded. " Not quite."

" You're so bright this morning that I thought the problems had all vanished into thin air. How are you doing?"

" Nicely. Commission worth two hundred a week including expenses, with a handsome bonus, if we pull off the job."

" Phee-ew!" Richard whistled. " Financial wizard at work. The blonde?"

" No. Grenfell."

" The trouble with you," said Richard, " is that you're right too often. I'd have settled with Rhoda Grenfell for fifty a week and told you that without me Prince would go bankrupt." He glanced towards the door, as footsteps shuffled towards them. An old man came in, carrying a tea-tray; a man with a red nose and veiny cheeks which even the gloom couldn't hide. " Thanks, Dad," said Richard, and took the tray. " This is my brother."

" How are you?" asked Martin.

" Fine, thank you." The old man was freshly shaven, faded, grey. " I'm glad to meet Mr. Fane's brother, I'm sure. You'll have lots to talk about, I won't keep you."

He hurried out.

" One thing about Dad," said Richard, " he never talks for the sake of talking."

" How did you meet him?" asked Martin interestedly.

" Pretty daughter," said Richard. " Prettier and classier

than you'd think. Oh, all fair and above board, I'm a much-engaged man and all that." His fiancée was in America, and would be away for several months. "We met a few weeks ago, she's a Fane fan—the Maestro, I mean. I saw her home one night and made quite a hit with the family. Then to-day I wanted to skulk somewhere I knew the police wouldn't suspect, so I came here."

There was more to it than that; in due time he would probably explain. He had always made the most unlikely friends.

Martin poured out tea, while Richard sat back; Richard was feeling much better, or he would have made a show of pouring out himself. There was still something up his sleeve; he had a conjuror's blandness, but wasn't really happy.

"Any progress?" he asked.

"Not really. There's a new development."

"Oh," said Richard. His voice became flat; Martin thought that he was thinking of the thing that had driven him here. It didn't please him. "Ma Grenfell?"

Martin nodded.

Richard took his tea, sipped it, and said nothing. A van passed outside, the window shook, one of the pictures looked as if it would be shaken off its nail. After that, silence fell. Richard knew about the murder and wasn't eager to talk about it. Martin wished that the room was brighter, so that he could see his brother's expression.

"How did you know?" he asked.

Richard put down his cup, moistened his lips, and took out his cigarette-case. The moments seemed to drag. Martin didn't understand and most certainly didn't like this. He couldn't hurry Richard, but had to fight for patience.

Richard said deliberately, "I saw it done."

The words dropped into the room like stones thrown into a deep pool from a great height. The ripples went through the atmosphere, and seemed to knock against Martin's face with sharp painful slaps.

"Horrible," Richard said.

Mrs. Grenfell had been killed by a knife-thrust to the heart, according to Grenfell; and Richard claimed that he had seen it. Worse, Richard had thought it necessary to rush for cover. The atmosphere could hardly get worse, but something was necessary to break it.

Martin sipped his tea.

" Was it a man or woman ? "

" Oh, a man," Richard said. " Little chap."

" Get a good look at him ? "

" Not really. He had a scarf over his face. I'd never recognise him again. Swine of a business."

Martin nodded pointlessly.

" She was in bed," said Richard. " Sitting up. So terrified she couldn't move, couldn't shout. She knew what was coming, of course—saw death on the way. I hope to heaven I never see anything like it again."

" Bad," said Martin. He felt the effect, could almost imagine it happening—and he could guess how it had affected his brother. He had to bring things nearer to normal, or Richard would live too much in that macabre scene. " Another cup ? "

" Er—thanks," said Richard, and held his cup out. " Bless your cotton socks, you know what to say, don't you ? " He laughed ; there wasn't much amusement in the sound, but it was a relief from tension. " Everyone else, with the possible exception of the Maestro, would have asked me why I didn't stop it."

" Probably." Martin poured out. " Why didn't you ? "

" I was on the floor. Unconscious, they thought."

" They ? "

" There were two of them. I didn't get a good look at the other chap, either—more scarfs ! He was a big lout." Richard rubbed his chin gingerly. " I've never been hit harder. Damned awful thing about it was that although I could see her face and actually saw that knife go in, I—— " He caught his breath, then made himself go on, " I couldn't do anything. Know what it's like when you just come round from being knocked out, don't you ? Numb, kind of. I was like that. Conscious but paralytic, so to speak. No doubt they thought I was dead to the world."

" Odd thing that they left you there," said Martin.

" Not really," said Richard. " They didn't have a chance not to. I was by the bathroom door, which was open. They'd been in there. After the little man killed her, they started to search. Forced a couple of locks. They didn't say anything, behaved just as if they'd given her a whiff of chloroform or something, to make her sleep. There she was, leaning back on the pillows, blood spreading over her night-dress. A white one. It was done, and I couldn't undo it. They'd taken my gun—damned good thing for me they didn't use it. Afraid of making a noise, I suppose. They thought I was right out, for a while. I edged towards the bathroom door, and then nipped in. It didn't take me a week to lock that door. It was one of those small, window-less bathrooms, with only one door. I was scared stiff in case they tried to smash that down. That's what it did to me, Scoop—scared me so badly that I hadn't any guts left. That was bad enough, by itself."

" For once you had some sense," Martin said. "If you'd tried to get them—— "

" Curtains. I know. I've never felt less valorous. In future I shall blame it on to shock and claim that I wasn't myself." Richard was striving to become his normal self. " Anyhow, they didn't try to get in. I stayed there for twenty minutes or so, I suppose, and then plucked up courage to unlock the door. They'd gone. She was lying just as I'd seen her, except that there was more red on her night-dress. It was about five o'clock, and I couldn't make up my mind what to do. No use to her, was I ? I had a half-baked idea that the precious pair might think that I'd seen enough of them to identify them, which might be useful, later on. I could have called the police, of course, but—— "

" Good thing you didn't," said Martin.

" Really think so, or just buttering me ? "

" Oh, I think so." Martin began to fill his pipe. " The police would have wanted to know how you came to be there, and you'd probably be on the suspect list. Just as well to keep off it. We're doing the job for Grenfell, too, and we don't have to hold hands with the police all the time." He talked much as Richard would have.

" Thanks," said Richard fervently. " I sneaked out. No one saw me, I'm pretty sure of that. Before I left I had a look round. They'd taken a lot of stuff out of the drawers, I should think, and they'd found a wall-safe and the com-bination. It was cleaned right out. I almost came back to the flat. But they'd taken my keys, I didn't want to call you out of bed——"

" Easy," said Martin. " You'd have lugged me out cheerfully. Why not come home ? "

Richard shrugged. " The man you can't deceive! Fact is, Scoop, I wanted time to think, and I didn't want to risk chatting with the police until I'd recovered. I knew they'd be at the flat or the office pretty soon—probably would, anyhow—and in that mood I wasn't sure I could face them and get away with anything. So I came here. No one could possibly guess I'd be here. I knew the family got up early, June has a couple of husky brothers who leave the house at six, for work. With my well-known charm I gained sanctuary."

" Hmm. And that's the lot ? "

" Hang it," protested Richard, " I did *some*thing worth boasting about. I've only related the sad tale of my failures so far. To tell you the truth, I was pretty sore last night. With you. And those damned women had made a fool of me, so I wasn't myself. I decided to have a cut at Rhoda's mother, she seemed a good bet. I left about four o'clock and went straight to the flat—got the address out of the telephone directory. After that course of lock-picking I took, a Yale meant nothing to me. I had the front door open in about three minutes. I thought everything was fine. When I was inside, though, I thought of you."

" Thanks," Martin grimaced.

" I'm serious. You'd have started working out the advantages of getting in before actually doing the job. I had vague notions of scaring the wits out of Rhoda or Mrs. Grenfell, and making them tell me what the trouble was. Also of having a look round for any papers that might have given us an idea. As a matter of fact," Richard added with a touch of defiance, " I wasn't so March-hared as it seems."

" Could have worked," said Martin musingly. " If you'd picked up some information about them—almost anything would have done—and confronted Rhoda with it this morning, she would have conceded us second sight, and been easier to handle. That was the general idea, I suppose."

" Yes. Thanks."

" Pleasure ! " Martin lit his pipe, and took his time over

it. "Now the real danger is that someone might have seen you. I doubt if they'd recognise you, but it's surprising how the police pick up suspects from slight descriptions. Feel pretty confident that you weren't seen?"

"Yes."

"Feel fit to drive?" asked Martin.

"I'm not on my last legs yet," said Richard. "Why?"

"I think it would be a good idea if you were to go down to Dorset. You could tell the Maestro what's on, he's always a possible for bright ideas. When the police get round to wondering what part we're playing in *l'affaire* Grenfell I can tell them you've gone down to consult Dad, and they won't be surprised at that. You can be back to-night, or to-morrow, and you won't miss much."

Richard said slowly, "Not a bad idea. I shan't be much use to any one to-day."

"Better not drive," said Martin decidedly. "You can catch the ten-thirty from Waterloo, I'll ring Dad and tell him to send the car to Bournemouth for you. You'll get a rest that way, and be there quicker. You needn't change until you get home—the girl's father can lend you a razor, I suppose."

"Oh, I can get a shave," said Richard. "Can't say I enthuse over the idea, but you're probably right. Mind telling me what's happened your end?"

"You need to know," said Martin.

.   .   .   .   .

He drove away, half an hour later, leaving Richard fully primed about what had happened. He didn't let himself think too much about what Richard had seen; the implications would become clear when the facts had seeped deeply enough into his mind. Richard was no longer an urgent problem, and thus far he felt relieved. Richard had saved him a great deal of trouble, and he had a lead over the police, knew more than if he had been at the dead woman's flat since her body had been found.

No one appeared to be watching 15 The Grove.

He drove the car back to the garage, then went by taxi to the parking-place where Richard had left the Buick—some distance away from Mrs. Grenfell's home. He drove back to the flat and put the car on the parking-plot. No one seemed to be taking any interest in the flat; he told himself there was no reason why they should.

He walked round to Quill House and up the stairs. As he opened the office door he heard the receptionist saying:

" No, I'm sorry, I've no idea when he'll be in."

He went in. The broad shoulders and fair head of Detective Sergeant Wimple of New Scotland Yard hid the receptionist from view. So every one had been right; the police hadn't taken long to get round to Prince.

9

WIMPLE TALKS

" HALLO, Sergeant," Martin said, and Wimple turned round quickly.

The pretty face of Jessica, the young receptionist, was flushed. She was never at ease when talking to policemen; all her life she had been taught to distrust them.

" Good morning, Mr. Fane." Wimple smiled.

" 'Morning," echoed Jessica. She was more beautiful than pretty; seventeen; and until her father had started to work for Prince, she had never known security.

" Hallo, Jessie. If any one calls, say I won't be free this morning. If any one wants Mr. Richard, he won't be in to-day—he's gone down to Dorset. Miss Marrison might come—if she telephones, I'll speak to her, of course."

" Yes, sir."

Martin led Wimple to his office. The detective took the chair which Martin had sat in while talking to Grenfell; and he filled it. He was a young man, not yet thirty, fair-skinned and with corn-coloured hair, a stolid, solid-looking man with more than a touch of imagination and a comforting gleam in his blue eyes. Yet he could look dull. A few months earlier the Fane brothers had rescued him from a nasty death; that made him a friend at court.

Martin pushed a box of cigarettes across the desk.

" No, thanks," said Wimple. " I'm trying to cut down—

don't smoke until after lunch.   Er—is that girl always like that ? "

" Girl ?   Oh, Jessie.   Like what ? "   Martin hadn't expected that opening, but was glad of it ; he could think about what he would say to Wimple.

" Every time I come in, she colours up and looks as if she'd like to drop through a hole in the floor."

Martin smiled.   " Oh, that's only her act for policemen. She does the rest of the job well."

" She ought to get over that silly attitude," Wimple said, as if it were a personal grievance.   " We haven't worried her old man since he started to work for you, and we gave him plenty of breaks before that.   She makes me feel a heel." Wimple frequently gave evidence of being a human being. He squared his shoulders : huge shoulders.   " You know what I've come about, I suppose."

Martin shrugged.   " Mrs. Grenfell ? "

" Yes.   Who told you about it ? "

" Sir Edward Grenfell."

" You're doing a job for him, aren't you ? " asked Wimple.

" Yes."

" No reason why you shouldn't," said Wimple.   " Look here, Mr. Fane, I don't want to see you get yourself in a jam.   Nor does the Chief.   So I've come round to find out what you know about this Grenfell business.   How long you've been working for Grenfell, all that kind of thing. Nothing formal, we just want to know."

" No reason why you shouldn't," said Martin.   " Rhoda Grenfell came along and told me she was worried about her mother and wanted me to find out what was troubling her. Grenfell turned up afterwards and told me he thought both women were worried, there was something he didn't understand going on, they wouldn't confide in him, and would I find out what it was all about ? "   He was filling his pipe as he talked, and looking squarely into Wimple's eyes.   " I turned the girl down at first, and then decided to see what I could do."

" Before or after the murder ? "

Martin said, " After.   But I'd have taken her on, in any case.   Grenfell made it worth while."

" I see," said Wimple, and deliberated.   " Don't take me

wrong, Mr. Fane. I know Prince hasn't been doing too
well lately, and Grenfell's worth money, but do you think
you're wise to get yourself mixed up in a murder investigation ? "

" I don't know yet."

" Bound to bring you up against us," said Wimple. " It
won't do any good if we clash, will it ? You might get a bit
of cash, but if it put you in bad at the Yard, in the long run
you'd be sorry."

Martin looked solemn.

" I'd hate to get in bad with the Yard." His eyes smiled,
and a responding gleam shone in Wimple's. If this had been
meant as a formal interview, Wimple wouldn't have come
alone. " What's all this about, Wimp ? Oakes send you
along to try to squeeze me out and make sure I'm not a
nuisance ? "

" Put it that way if you like," said Wimple. " The Chief
has a soft spot for you, but he knows you and that young rip
Richard are capable of going haywire. He doesn't want a
clash. This is an ugly job. Not your kind of thing at all—
he says."

" What does he think ? "

" Don't ask me," said Wimple.

" Well, I don't see any reason for being frightened off yet,"
Martin said.

" Didn't think you would," said Wimple. " But there's
an angle you might not know, Mr. Fane. How well do you
know this girl Rhoda Grenfell ? "

" I've met her three times."

" What do you make of her ? "

" Some sense, more money, badly spoiled," said Martin
promptly.

" Not far wrong," said Wimple thoughtfully. " Take it
from me, she's not a fool. We've had our eyes on her and
the Kennedy woman for some time. Know Kennedy ? "

" Slightly."

" You're not the kind to fall for a fortune-teller, anyhow,"
said Wimple. " We don't know what it's all about, but
several people who've believed in horoscopes and all that
kind of thing have burned their fingers badly lately. They've
all known Hilda Kennedy, too. They've lost a lot of money.

None of them has admitted it, but you know how we pick up information. We collected enough to wonder what Kennedy's up to."

Martin frowned, but didn't speak. Wimple seemed to think that he had said enough for the time being, and waited. The telephone bell rang in the outer office, and Jessica's clear young voice, with its faintly Cockney accent, came clearly through the wooden partition.

" Prince Agency. . . . No, I'm sorry, Mr. Fane's not free this morning, can I take a message ? . . . Yes . . . Yes . . . Thank you, I'll tell him."

The bell tinged as she rang off.

" Up to what ? " asked Martin. " Fleecing the credulous ? "

" That's about it. If we're right, a lot of young people go and see Hilda K., who tells them how to invest their money. They take her advice, and it goes down the drain. Most of them seem to think it's the world that's gone wrong, not Hilda K. She manages to give them implicit faith in her. We haven't managed to get a single one to say a word against her or admit they invested on her say-so."

" Perhaps they didn't," said Martin.

Wimple wrinkled his nose. " Don't think there's much doubt. They all know her, all visit her, all have private sessions with her, all think that she's gifted with second sight. Almost worship her. Personal magnetism, I suppose, but I wouldn't go across the street to look in her eyes. She's a hypnotist, too."

" Full of accomplishments," murmured Martin.

" Oh, she's got her head screwed on," said Wimple. " Add it up, Mr. Fane. She gets influence over these people, they invest big money and lose it. It nearly always works the same way—they buy shares at a good price, and the bottom drops out of the market. We haven't been able to prove that the market's rigged, it all seems genuine enough, and some mugs have to lose. Funny thing so many of her friends do, isn't it ? "

" Could be," conceded Martin. " Is there any evidence that Hilda Kennedy collects ? "

" Not yet."

Martin said, " You haven't exactly got her ready for the dock, have you ? "

" She's smart," said Wimple. " Slippery, too. She might be too smart for us. She wouldn't be the first who's run a racket without giving herself away. Not the first we've known about without getting evidence, either. But things look like warming up, don't they ? With the murder, I mean. We can grill Hilda K. a lot better now—in fact, we've never been able to do much before, but she's been bad friends with Mrs. Grenfell for months. They've had a couple of rows."

" I can see you gloating," murmured Martin.

" She's at the Yard now, with the Chief," said Wimple. " So's Rhoda G. We'd take it for granted Rhoda G. was being prepared for the plucking, except that she's been with Hilda K. too long. Half a dozen others have lost a pile since they've strung along together. Any reason to think that Rhoda G. or her mother were short of cash ? "

" Her bag's always over-flowing with pound notes, and as Richard would say, she dresses like a million pounds. No."

" Funny business," said Wimple. " Well, this might blow up into something big. The Chief thought you ought to be warned."

" And said that if I kept anything to myself, I'd buy myself a packet of trouble," Martin said dryly.

Wimple grinned. " That's about it ! I told him he needn't worry, you wouldn't go asking for it. Why's your brother gone down to Dorset, by the way ? " He didn't seem interested in the question ; Wimple talked too much, or seemed to, and slipped apparently insignificant questions and comments into the general flow.

" To see the family—and try to borrow some money, I shouldn't wonder."

" Still at it ? " asked Wimple. " He's a caution ! Can't help liking him, can you ? What's happened to his girl friend, that film actress ? Kathleen something—Wilder, that's it."

" Hollywood."

" Good lord ! That's finished that, then."

" Only one film," said Martin, " and judging from her letters, she'll be home on the first 'plane she can catch. Why ? "

" Oh, nothing."

" Why ? " repeated Martin firmly.

Wimple grinned.

" None of my business," he said. " I happened to be out Fulham way last week, had a job there. Read about it ? Woman murdered her husband by smothering him with a pillow. Took me out there most days, and I saw Richard twice, with a pretty little bit of skirt. Shook me, rather, the last time I saw him he was all for Kathleen Wilder."

" He still is," said Martin.

" I shouldn't think Kathleen would like it, but what the eye doesn't see the heart doesn't grieve about, I suppose." Wimple stood up. " Time I was going, I've been here too long already. If you pick anything up, you'll let us know, won't you ? Might as well compare notes."

" Yes," said Martin. " But just a minute. Keep your voice low." He nodded towards the door, indicating Jessica. " What's this about Richard ? Sure you're right ?"

" Mightn't be anything in it," said Wimple, " but I saw him. Checked up on the girl, too—you know how it is, can't help checking. She's all right. So's the family. At first I thought Richard might be working for Prince, but I shouldn't think so, with that crowd. Not exactly the kind of family your father would like him to get in with, though. *Or* Mrs. Fane."

Martin forced a laugh. " No. I'm glad you told me. Fulham job finished ? "

" All sewn up," said Wimple. " I must run along, Mr. Fane."

Martin saw him out; and saw, also, that Jessica's face went red when Wimple looked across at her and took the trouble to wish her good morning. She muttered under her breath. Martin didn't spend much time thinking about Jessica's reaction to a Yard man. Little worrying things nagged at him; the fact that Richard had been recognised in Fulham, might have been pointed out to members of the Fulham force—and, consequently, might have been seen and recognised that morning. If a report reached Wimple there would be inquiries. He tried to shrug the possibility off; it wasn't easy.

Wimple had given him plenty to think about, apart from that. He wouldn't have told the story of Hilda Kennedy and Rhoda for the sake of it. The Yard had good reason for wondering what the two women were up to. Last night they had come near to quarrelling, had both been on edge.

The telephone bell rang in the outer office. Jessica answered and her voice warmed:

"Good morning, Miss. Yes, he's in, he said put you through." Martin's bell rang, and he took the receiver off quickly: this would be Barbara.

Barbara was still at her flat, and wanted to come into the office. She was feeling quite fit, she said, and if Martin and Richard were going to be out a lot, she was needed at Quill House. Would he be in if she came round at once?

"I suppose you'd better," said Martin. "Sure you're fit?"

"I'm perfectly all right," said Barbara. "Don't try to wrap me in cotton-wool, darling. I'll be round in half an hour." She rang off, but voices continued—from the other room. Martin had heard them, off-stage, as it were; now he listened more intently.

"Well, he's not," Jessica said.

A man spoke, with a laugh in his voice.

"But I heard him talking. I'll just sit and wait until he shows up, and then have a word with him."

"It's no use," said Jessica, annoyed. "When he says he's not free, he—here! Where are you going?"

The man laughed. "Sitting and waiting! Sorry, but I must see him."

Martin sat back and watched the door. Jessica's footsteps scurried across the room, but before she could reach the door, it opened. A tall, sallow-faced, handsome young man came in, smiling broadly. He had good white teeth, was well dressed, and walked with a grace that was almost a swagger.

He had met Rhoda Grenfell when she had left Matten's office in Arundel Street.

10

MAN OF ACTION

THE young man beamed.

"Mr. Martin Fane, I believe? *Alias* Prince. Good morning." He sauntered across the office, taking out a gold cigarette-case. "I fancied you were in. Mind if I sit down?"

He touched the back of the upholstered chair.

"Good morning," Martin said heavily. He stood up and rounded the desk as the young man sat down. He saw the head tilted, to look at him; the brown eyes, smiling, sardonic, but with just a hint of nervousness, the mobile face and rather lantern jaw, dark hair, smooth, sallow complexion. This young man probably fancied himself, and was almost certainly a great success with women. Martin let him light the cigarette and put the case away. Then he gripped his right arm and jerked him to his feet. The cigarette dropped.

"Here!"

Martin didn't speak, pulled the man's arm behind him in a hammer-lock and hustled him towards the door. He called to Jessica, "Open the door, please." She opened it and gaped as Martin bundled his caller to the outer door and then dived, fawn-like, towards that and opened it. Martin propelled the young man outside and let him go. He went back, closed the door firmly, and smiled at a gaping Jessica.

"We must make him understand that we mean what we say, mustn't we?"

"Oo, yes!" Jessica waved a hand towards the door, and thus dismissed the caller and the subject. She had the Cockney's supreme self-confidence and native ability to change swiftly with the circumstances. "Dad's ever so sorry, Mr. Martin, but his leg's still bad. Can't hardly stand on it. The doctor says he's got to stay in bed for at least another three days. Cursing something awful, Dad is."

"Tell him not to be a fool," said Martin.

"I told him," said Jessica. "I said you'd understand."

"I'll look round and see him," promised Martin.

Rennie, Jessica's father, was the only other active worker at Prince outside the family; Barbara was considered one of the family. Rennie was a tough, chunky Cockney who knew the inside of jail, whom life had given a raw deal—a fact conceded even at Scotland Yard. He had given Prince information on an earlier case, become involved, and been cleared of suspicion. At that time Martin and Barbara had discovered his passionate devotion to his only child—Jessica.

Prince had needed staff, and the Rennies had been engaged. In different ways, both were invaluable.

"He'll be glad to see you," Jessica said.

There was a tap at the door. Martin waited, Jessica called, "Come in". The tall young man entered, no longer smiling but still impressively handsome. He went straight to Jessica, without looking at Martin, and said quietly :

"I'll leave my card. When Mr. Fane's free, ask him if he'll give me an appointment as quickly as possible, will you ? It's about Miss Grenfell. I'll write her name down." He took a card from his pocket, a pencil from another.

Martin said, "I can manage ten minutes or so now."

"Oh. Good. Thanks." The young man handed Martin the card. He was Reginald Fraser, of 1 Mount Court, Mayfair.

"Put that on the records, Jessie," Martin said, handing over the card.

The two men walked to his office. Martin rounded the desk and motioned to the upholstered chair. Reginald Fraser sat down, and Martin pushed the box of cigarettes across the desk, and began to fill his own pipe.

"Thanks. Rhoda's told me that she's been to see you, and what she's said. I met her in Arundel Street. She'd told Hilda Kennedy where she was going, and I tried to catch her up."

"Why ?" asked Martin.

"I wasn't a bit sure she was wise to let you have a hand in the job," said Fraser frankly. "While things were normal it didn't matter, but after her mother's murder, I thought it was a matter for the police and no one else. Murder isn't an amateur's job. I could see Rhoda getting herself into a lot of trouble with the police, and wanted to stop it."

"Praiseworthy," murmured Martin.

"I thought so. I'm not sure now." Fraser smiled a little. "You didn't stand much nonsense from her, I gather. Rhoda's sound enough, but she's so used to having her own way that it's doing her a lot of harm." His smile widened. "And you'll be telling yourself that she's not the only one too used to getting everything asked for ! "

Martin waved his pipe. "Forget it."

" I thought I'd come and find out what you make of the situation," said Fraser.

" I haven't had much time to sort it out." Martin lit the pipe, and took his time doing it. " Boiled down, her mother was frightened, Rhoda blamed that on to resentment at being neglected, and now she knows there was more to it. Her mother warned her that she might be in danger, and now Rhoda's wondering if she is. I suppose there could be something in it."

" That's what worries me," said Fraser. " Are you going to try to find out ? "

" I'm not collecting any fee from her, if that's what you mean."

Fraser grinned. " No. That's what made me think you might be on the up-and-up. On the other hand, by refusing a fee, you might simply be playing safe—dropping the case, without letting her know what you're doing. Is that what you're up to ? "

" No."

" Any prospect of finding the truth ? "

" Not yet."

" I see," said Fraser. He stubbed out his cigarette and immediately lit another. " Now that it's murder, the police won't let the grass grow under their feet. They'll probably get there a long time before you do, but—— " He hesitated, weighing his words and then went on carefully, " If you think I can help, will you tell me ? "

Martin pondered.

Fraser went on eagerly, " I want to. I'm—I'm in love with Rhoda." He coloured slightly. " Seriously. I want to get her out of any trouble she's in. There's another thing I want to do, too, and this may be the opportunity. I want to get her away from that feminine Old Moore, Hilda Kennedy. She isn't doing Rhoda any good. It's no use being ruthless, though, and I'm trying to finesse a bit. If I try to make Rhoda drop the old hag, Rhoda will cling tighter. If I can prove that Hilda's a charlatan, and let Rhoda find it out for herself, I think it'll work the trick. Rhoda's no fool."

" Right tactics, I should say," murmured Martin.

" Thanks. I won't take up any more of your time."

Fraser stood up quickly. He looked physically fit, even though he was too thin. " I've proved you're a man of action, anyhow ! "

" If I'd let you get away with that, the girl wouldn't know how to handle people who come when I'm busy," said Martin dryly.

Fraser smiled, and Martin saw him into the outer office. Fraser nodded to Jessica, who gave him a cool stare, and went out. Jessica's eyes dropped to the card she was making out—listing Reginald Fraser. If Barbara were here, she could start finding out what there was to know about that young man. She was late; ought to be here by now. He checked; it was more than half an hour since she had said she would come right away, and she lived only twenty minutes from Quill House. He often felt uneasy about Richard, but never so quickly as about the possibility of trouble for Barbara. He was restless for the next five minutes, then heard her coming up the stairs.

She came in, looking fresh-faced; the cold had stung her cheeks and reddened them, and put an added sparkle in her eyes. Nothing suggested that she was feeling the after-effects of her bout of 'flu.

He kissed her.

" Office hours, Scoop ! "

" That's right." He kissed her again, and she laughed and pulled herself free. She wore a three-quarter-length seal coat and a small hat of the same fur. She took this off and poked her fingers through her hair; she could do that and not make her hair look as if it hadn't been brushed for days.

" Anything new ? "

" Yes, my sweet. We've had a visitor . . ."

He told her about Fraser; and arranged for her to find out what she could about the young man, about Hilda Kennedy, and the Grenfells. Barbara had hosts of acquaintances in London, including many in Fleet Street; no one could sit at the end of a telephone and learn more. She would get facts, too—sort them out of the mass of gossip which would flood her ears.

He told her about Richard.

She frowned.

"I think he'll cool his heels at home for a day or two," Martin said. "What he saw this morning really shook him. I'm a bit worried, in case he was recognised and the Yard gets to know of it. On the other hand, they'll probably assume that it's an *affaire*, and think nothing more of it."

Barbara said slowly, "*Is* it an *affaire* ? "

"I haven't seen any signs," said Martin. "I haven't known him lose his head since Kathleen came along, either ! I thought he'd really steadied. If this girl's attractive he might be playing the fool, although I wouldn't like to think so."

"It's a thousand pities Kathleen took that Hollywood offer," Barbara frowned.

"Oh, I don't know. If he can hold out for the six months we'll know that it's the real thing. If he falls by the way— well, I'd be sorry. Kathleen's as nice as they come, but it will save them wrecking the marriage later."

"I suppose so," said Barbara. "Haven't you seen this girl at Fulham ? "

"No."

"Pity Rennie's laid up," mused Barbara. "He'd find out what there is to know about that family, and he'd soon know just what's happening between the girl and Richard. We didn't want this added complication just when a big job's turned up. What do you make of things, Scoop ? "

Martin said thoughtfully, "I don't much like it. I'm not convinced we've heard everything that Grenfell can tell us, and I'm doubtful whether Rhoda's come clean. I'm thinking of making a frontal attack on Hilda Kennedy. I've been wondering why Wimple came—— " He broke off, to tell her all that Wimple had said, and went on, "He admitted that Oakes sent him. I doubt if Oakes would do that without talking to Superintendent Kelby first, you know how they work together. I could take the surface view that they came to put us off the case—— " He paused, for Barbara gave a smothered laugh. "What's up ? "

"I was trying to imagine you taking the surface view ! "

"Be serious. Or we could take it that Kelby and Oakes know perfectly well we can't be frightened off and there's no reason why we shouldn't go on with the case. That means they had another reason for sending Wimple. He let out plenty about Hilda Kennedy, pointed her out as the likely villain of the piece, but admitted they couldn't prove a thing against her. That could have been to divert me from other lines and make me go for Hilda in a big way. Couldn't it ? "

Barbara nodded.

" Or it could be that they want me to goad Hilda—on the theory that if I goad her she might do something silly and lay herself open to attack from them. If I go for Hilda, we'll give them that chance, anyhow."

" That's the way the Maestro would work," said Barbara.

" Oh, in a book, yes." Martin laughed. " The more I sit back and watch myself working, the more I realise how Dad and Prince influence me. I seem to think the way Dad makes his hero think ! The odd thing is, it often comes off. I think I'll go and see Hilda. That's what Grenfell wants me to do, too. He pointed a finger at Hilda—more than a finger, if it comes to that—and Rhoda made me understand how her mother and Grenfell quarrelled. That makes Grenfell as interesting as Hilda, doesn't it ? " He heard the telephone bell ring in the outer office. " And I'd better be off, or something will crop up to stop me." The desk telephone rang. " You see." He lifted the telephone. " Hallo ? "

" It's your father," said Jessica breathlessly ; talking to Jonathan Fane always affected her like that. " You're through."

" Scoop ? " Jonathan Fane's deep voice came clearly.

" Hal-*lo*, Dad ! "

" At least you sound as if you're pleased to hear me," said Fane. " I suppose that's as much as I can expect. Scoop, I haven't much time, I don't want your mother to hear about this. What's the trouble ? "

" Trouble ? "

" Don't hedge."

" I've a biggish job, but I don't know anything about trouble—yet. Richard got into a jam, but he's out of it. Why ? "

He could imagine his father, big, burly, sitting at his huge desk in the lovely Dorset house, typewriter pushed away from him, manuscript pages neatly in front of him, and turned towards the window with the telephone at his ear. He would be smoking and screwing up his right eye, because the smoke from a cigarette was getting into it, beneath his horn-rimmed glasses.

" I had a telephone call twenty minutes ago. A man warned me to get you out of London, and rang off. Said you were to keep clear of a woman named Rhoda Grenfell. If your mother heard of it, she'd go scatty. I wanted to make sure everything was all right. I—just a minute, I think she's coming in." There was a pause; then Fane spoke again. " It's all right, she's gone into the bedroom. What's this about Richard ? "

" He'll be down this afternoon—can you send the car to Dorchester to pick him up from the ten-thirty from Waterloo ? "

" Don't tell me he's on the run," said Fane anxiously.

Martin laughed.

" No. He'll tell you all about it. Warn Mother that he was hit over the head last night, he'll sport some sticking plaster on."

" All right. Now I must ring off, or—— "

" Just a minute! How well do you know Grenfell of the *Sunday Clarion* ? "

" Sensible chap," said Fane promptly. " Almost the only newspaper which still runs a serial every week ! " He laughed. " I don't know him really well, but he's all right. Why ? "

" The job's for him."

" I shouldn't think there's anything to worry about with Grenfell," said Fane. " Now I really must go, or—— "

A new voice broke in: his wife's.

" Or *I'll* be wondering who you're talking to and why you're being so mysterious about it," said Evelyn Fane tartly. " *I* happened to be by the other telephone and picked it up to make a call. So I've heard everything, *darling*, it's no use trying to fob me off with a lot of half-truths."

Martin chuckled.

For once Jonathan Fane was speechless.

" It's not funny," said Evelyn, still tartly. " And I know one thing, when Richard's here he'll stay here. If he's been hurt, I won't let him come back to London and get mixed up in a lot of beastly crime. That's definite."

"You deal with Richard," said Martin brightly. "It's more than I can. I'll be down as soon as I can. 'Bye."

His mother and father answered in unison. He rang off, smiling: the occasional clashes at home, and his father's constant and usually futile attempts to shelter his mother from things she wouldn't like, always amused him. He doubted whether she had heard about the man who had telephoned a warning; she wouldn't have been able to keep that to herself. He fingered his pipe as he told Barbara what had happened. He didn't expect Barbara to comment on the man who had taken the trouble to telephone Jonathan Fane.

She said, "Are you still going to see Hilda Kennedy?"

"Right away," said Martin, and jumped up.

He left the office five minutes afterwards, and drove straight to Lingham Court.

11 THE STAR-GAZER

MARTIN pulled up outside the block of flats and walked to the entrance where he had gone the night before. A different commissionaire spoke to him.

"I know my way, thanks."

He could have gone in the lift; he preferred to walk. As he walked, thoughts which had been vague on the way here crystallised. He was being pushed around. Richard would have expressed it more pithily. He had taken some time awakening to the fact, and couldn't avoid it now. He'd done nothing, except rescue Richard from a foolish plight. He'd sat in the flat or the office while others had made things happen to him. He was as much a detective as the commissionaire downstairs.

He found himself smiling faintly.

He could imagine his father's characters musing in much the same way. Everything he had said to Barbara about the Maestro and Prince was true.

He reached the flat and rang the bell. Nothing happened. He rang again. Probably she was out and the flat empty. She might still be at the Yard. If he had followed Richard's example and taken a course in picking locks from a locksmith who ought to have known better, he would be able to laugh at this lock. Richard would have laughed. The easiest way he could force entry was by battering a door down. Richard was much more subtle; that was the difference between the two. He woke to the fact that he was missing Richard's help, and not simply his company. Richard was full of bright ideas, and occasionally one of them was a winner.

He rang again.

He was startled when the door opened.

" Yes ? " a little woman whispered.

She was very small; didn't quite come up to his shoulder. She looked up at him, her heart-shaped face pale, her eyes enormous. There was nothing of her; she was as flat-chested as Hilda Kennedy. She wore a black dress and a white apron, but no cap. Her dark hair was plastered down the sides of her face and across her forehead, making a frame.

" Miss Kennedy, please," said Martin.

" Oh, no ! " The little woman seemed distressed. " Oh, no, I can't disturb her."

" I won't keep her long." Martin put a foot round the door.

" Oh, *please*," breathed the maid, but she backed away. Martin thought of Fraser, and what had happened to him when he had thrust himself where he wasn't wanted. " Don't do anything to disturb her."

" All right," said Martin.

He went in, and closed the door. The maid seemed incapable of making a decision and stood watching him, wringing her hands. Her tiny stature startled him, even now. He couldn't take his gaze away from her.

" What's the matter ? "

" She's *busy*."

They were in a squarish hall; Martin hadn't taken much notice of it the night before. The walls were plainly painted, but here and there stars glistened like silver; large stars and small. Stars decorated two mirrors and several pieces of furniture, too. All the doors except one were closed; the open door showed a kitchen.

"Hasn't she been out?" asked Martin.

"Yes, yes." The maid fluttered. She was an elfin creature, with her startlingly black hair and pallid face and enormous eyes. "The police made her go with them, she's only been back half an hour, she's been *busy* ever since."

"How long will she be?"

"Oh, I don't know. I *never* know."

Since Martin had first seen her, his voice had been muted; he had thought that she was whispering so as to make sure that her mistress wasn't disturbed. He wasn't sure now. Her natural voice was a whispering one. She wasn't quite real.

"Do you mean she's writing?"

"Oh, *no*."

"Then what—— "

"She's *gazing*," said the maid.

Martin gulped.

"Which room?"

"Oh, please—— "

He looked round, recognised the door of the room where he had been with Richard; there were three others, all closed. He went towards the nearest, opened it, and saw a bedroom. He closed that, and tried the next. The little maid wrung her hands pathetically, but made no further attempt to stop him.

The door opened.

It was a small room; and dark. That startled him. Black curtains were drawn, shutting out all daylight. Yet he could see points of light on the walls; stars. After a few moments he made out a sitting figure.

Hilda Kennedy sat at a small table in front of a star on a pedestal; staring, as a gypsy might stare into a crystal. The star glistened a silvery colour; seemed to glow. There were smaller stars in it, reflections from those on the walls.

There was silence in the room.

Martin stepped inside and closed the door. Light had come in from the hall, but the woman at the table appeared to have noticed nothing. Now that he was more accustomed to the gloom, Martin could make out her profile. Long, pointed chin; long nose; high forehead. He hadn't noticed her profile the night before, yet it was much more striking than her full face.

He imagined that her eyes were glowing.

He went a little nearer, so that he could see what she was looking at. All he could see were stars inside the star; and they were moving.

The maid was unreal; the stars were unreal; everything here was unreal. Yet he felt its effect—like something which got into him and began to make his nerves tingle. He fancied that the hair on the back of his neck was rising, as if there were forces here beyond his understanding.

Absurd?

He stood quite still, watching those small stars moving within the large one; tiny points of brilliant light which shimmered and twinkled, like the stars of the sky. He knew that he was breathing with bated breath. He wished he weren't here; he didn't want to disturb the woman. Yet he couldn't make himself move.

Time seemed to fade.

He did not know how long he had been there when the woman moved. He heard a rustle of sound, then saw her turn her head; the light was good enough for him to see her eyes, and the way she looked at him.

She said, " What is it ? "

Her voice was empty with the emptiness of weariness, of utter fatigue. It wasn't even faintly like the shrill and quarrelsome voice he had heard the night before.

He said, " I want to talk to you, Miss Kennedy."

He couldn't put any vigour into his voice, was afraid that if she said that she hadn't time, he would turn away and leave her. Before she dismissed him, he began to key himself up to resist. He rebelled against the idea that atmosphere could influence him like this.

" About what ? " Her voice was the same.

" Mrs. Grenfell."

" I can tell you nothing about Mrs. Grenfell. Who are you ? Another policeman ? "

Had she asked that question the previous night, she would have said the word " policeman " with a sneer. Now she just uttered it as if she weren't really interested.

She might not recognise his face in that gloom. Didn't she recognise his voice?

" I'm Martin Fane."

" Fane," she said. " Fane. Oh, yes. Rhoda has seen you, hasn't she? I can't do any more. I've done everything I can to help the child, I can't do any more. She rejects all their advice. She won't listen to them."

Some feeling crept into her voice; she uttered " them " as if it were a hallowed name.

" Whose advice? " he asked.

" Theirs," she said. " The guidance of the stars. If she won't listen, she must expect trouble. I can't help her any more. I can't help you. Don't stay."

He had passed the danger of turning away at her behest. He wished there were more light. He could back two paces and switch on the light, but felt reluctant to. It would bring reality into this unreal room. He wondered what it would look like, lit up, and realised that his thoughts were wandering at a time when he needed to concentrate desperately. He actually squared his shoulders.

" All this nonsense doesn't impress me." He spoke more roughly than he intended. " You're responsible for most of her troubles."

" *I* ? "

" Yes."

" Don't be a foolish young man," she said wearily. " You're as bad as young Fraser. He looks at me as if I were a Circe, and were going to turn her into a pig at any minute. Go away, with your silly ideas."

Martin turned round abruptly, but didn't go out. He reached the door, and could make out the dark shape of the light switches. He pressed them down. Light came on, but didn't flood the room. The lighting was concealed, running round the ceiling, soft, gentle. It shone on the dark curtains and the large silvery star; on the woman and on the stars which dotted the walls. The colouring was like that of a lovely sunset: soft blues, shading away into the darkness of purple; and along one wall the orange red of the setting sun's afterglow. There was beauty here.

The woman was sitting on a stool, wearing an ordinary tweed suit. Her eyes seemed dull now. She looked tired.

There were dark patches beneath her eyes. She had daubed lipstick on carelessly, and it was running at one corner, and she had powdered her face but hadn't used rouge.

" I can do nothing to help you," she said. " You would reject anything I offered. As she does. Go away."

" You know she's in danger."

" Of course she is."

" What makes you so sure ? "

" Isn't her mother lying dead—murdered ? "

" That needn't affect Rhoda."

" Oh, you fool," said Hilda Kennedy. " You fool."

She moved backwards slowly, reached the pedestal, and touched one side of it. Bright light came from the star; the room was filled with it. It wasn't dazzling, but had a crystal clearness that showed up everything and hardened the beauty of the colouring. It also hardened the woman's face. Last night he had guessed that she was nearer fifty than forty; now, he thought she might be sixty. All the lines and wrinkles at and beneath her chin, at her mouth and the corners of her eyes, showed up in criss-cross lines. Her face had been lifted, a long time ago. The powdered pallor made her look almost grotesque. Her eyes were dull, but not entirely without expression.

She studied Martin.

Under the cold appraisal he felt as if he were a specimen under a microscope. She was looking at him as coldly and dispassionately as any scientist. She didn't move, but her gaze travelled about his face. She was reading his thoughts, knew he was bluffing. Absurd ? It didn't seem so then.

" You're a nice young man," she said. " Go away and forget all about it."

Had she said that last night it would have been unbearably patronising. Instead, the words were like those of a wise old woman who was not interested in pride or patronage, was simply voicing her thoughts. She turned away from him and pressed the pedestal again; the light went out. She moved past him, towards the door, actually touched the handle before he turned.

He took her arm; it was thin, bony, cold; cold enough to surprise him, because the room was warm.

" Why is Rhoda Grenfell in danger ? "

"Don't worry me any more," she said.

"Why is Rhoda in danger? Why are you so sure?"

She moved her arm, and he let go. She stared at him, her face nothing like so lined and old in this kinder light. She smiled.

"It's in the stars," she said. "I warned her mother, I told her mother what to do. She ignored me. I read of her death, by violence, months before it happened. I know that Rhoda will die if she doesn't do what I tell her."

Martin felt prickles run up and down his spine.

"What did you tell her?"

"Go and ask *her*," said Hilda Kennedy.

12 HIGH HAND

MARTIN was on the point of turning away and giving the woman best. He actually moved. The streak of stubbornness in him came to his rescue. He took out his pipe and smoothed the bowl; that always seemed to help. He didn't shout or raise his voice, but both tone and words were biting.

"Not yet, Miss Kennedy, I haven't finished with you. I've had enough of this rigmarole. You may fool the addlepated, but you won't fool anyone who has an ounce of common sense. How did you know Mrs. Grenfell was in danger? Out with it—how did you *know*?"

The woman didn't answer.

Martin said, "You've had one session with the police, and you'll have more. They may pretend to believe you, but they don't. You know more than you ought about the murder. More about the danger to Rhoda. How did you find out?"

She stood still, silent, staring. That baffled him. He could have coped, had she tried to argue and justify herself; but the way she looked made him feel a fool.

He said, "The stars won't save you from being hanged. What did you tell Rhoda?"

Hilda Kennedy turned slowly, went to the stool, and sat

down. She looked into the big star, as if she had forgotten that Martin was in the room. Short of shaking her, there wasn't much he could do. He needed one single fact which would frighten her; and he hadn't got it.

At least, he must have a useful parting shot. Richard would have had a dozen, ready to roll off his tongue; Martin felt tongue-tied. As he watched, the woman seemed to withdraw from him. He saw the glow returning to her eyes.

He said, " Did the stars tell you how much it will cost Rhoda to get out of danger ? "

She took no notice; it was as if she wasn't there.

He turned and went out. The little maid fluttered between the front door and the middle of the hall, anxious and wide-eyed. She didn't speak. He strode to the door and went out, slamming it behind him; it didn't latch. He put his foot against it, but the maid didn't come to close it. He heard her feather-light footsteps.

He went back into the hall. The kitchen door was closed; the only one open was that of Hilda Kennedy's room. He tiptoed towards it, and peered inside. The room was in darkness again, and he could just make out her figure as she sat in front of the star, which radiated light. He judged that she had dismissed him from her mind as completely as if he had never been here.

He went out, closed the door firmly, and walked slowly to the head of the stairs. He was still being pushed around, and didn't like it. Some cases were simple; the big ones like this were different. As he walked down the stairs, he faced obvious but unpalatable facts. The police had every possible advantage over him. Before he could really start investigating, he had to know a lot more about all the people in the case.

He could get general and superficial knowledge, but wasn't yet near the undercurrents which mattered. He hadn't even a strong lead. It was like beating the air. He wondered what had possessed him to set up as an inquiry agent; some fanciful notion, put into his head through early reading of his father's books? It was flopping financially, and it wouldn't, if he really got results. He wouldn't touch the bread-and-butter of divorce cases. If he wanted to make a success of the job, he would have to forget his high " moral " tone. Detecting meant digging out dirt. As much dirt as he could find. If he wanted to make a go of Prince, he would have to soil his hands.

By the time he was at the wheel of the car he was able to think about Hilda Kennedy. If she had put up an act, she had completely fooled him. He'd left with much more respect for her sincerity than he'd had before. She believed in herself and her stars. Was there anything in it ? Astrology was as old as the hills.

He drove off.

He didn't know where to start next. High-handedness had failed him completely. He was under contract to Grenfell and was being well paid for it—and he hadn't any idea how to start earning the money. He was still in a position where he had to sit back and take whatever was thrown at him, he couldn't dictate any course of action. His mood was as glum as it could be when he reached the office.

Jessica smiled at him timidly ; she was nearly always timid. He mustn't forget that he had promised to go and see her father.

Barbara, typing from shorthand notes, looked up with an absent smile, finished the sentence she was on, and sat back.

" Hallo, darling. Did she crack ? "

" She's made of rubber," said Martin.

" Oh." Barbara frowned, looked at him straightly, and read his mood. She never failed to.

" Have you found anything ? " he asked.

" Not much," said Barbara. " Hilda Kennedy has a good reputation, I've talked to several people who have implicit faith in her. None of them has been cheated or lost any money through taking her advice. It rather scares me."

" Scares ? "

" That people should be guided by what she's supposed to read in the stars."

" Nothing new in that," said Martin carelessly, and sat on the corner of the desk. " What about Rhoda ? "

Barbara said, " It's interesting."

" How ? "

" Rhoda won a reputation for being the flightiest and

most frivolous member of the smart set," Barbara told him. " No viciousness—just no morals. Young man after young man. Gambling, drinking, anything for a good time. Then she met Hilda Kennedy and seemed to change.

" She quietened down, behaved almost decorously, and took on a steady young man. Reggie Fraser. She cut most of her old friends, dropped most of her old habits. Some put it down to true love and Reggie, most seem to think that it was Hilda Kennedy's influence."

" Oh," said Martin again. He put his pipe between his lips and lit it. He didn't notice the gloom fading; it just went.

" What's important about that ? " demanded Barbara.

" As if you didn't know ! "

" I don't."

" Surely it's obvious," said Martin. " Rhoda stops being wild and frivolous—and who protests ? If we can believe what we're told, her mother does. Mothers usually heave a sigh of relief when giddy daughters begin to settle down. Odd mother."

Barbara said, " Yes, of course."

" Either her mother was odd or she knew there was some-thing ugly behind the new influence at work on Rhoda," said Martin. " Everyone takes it for granted that the in-fluence was Hilda's, but it could have been Fraser's. What do we know about him ? "

" Practically nothing," said Barbara.

Martin waited.

" He's a man without a background," Barbara went on. " No one knows where he came from, where he was educated, anything about him. He appeared in London and started visiting the night-clubs, worked his way into a society set, had good manners and a lot of polish, and was a reasonable success. Then he met Rhoda. He hasn't looked at any one else since then, as far as I can find out."

" Money ? "

" He seems to have enough."

" Source ? "

" I haven't found out. I haven't had a lot of time, of course."

Martin smiled. " You've done wonders ! I think we

want to pay Reginald Fraser a lot of attention. Get him on the telephone, Bar. Ask him to come and see you, have a long and earnest talk, keep him here for at least an hour."

Barbara's eyes sparkled. " Going hunting ? "

" Yes."

" Be careful, darling."

Martin laughed.

. . . . .

Fraser was at his flat, and promised to come to Quill House at once.

. . . . .

The bad mood of the morning was over. Martin reached Fraser's flat half an hour after leaving the office, and knew he could trust Barbara to keep Fraser at the office for at least an hour ; he had that hour to play with. Mount Court was a mews with a high-sounding name, a little cul-de-sac behind one of the streets near Park Lane. The ground was cobbled, eighteenth-century stables had been turned into flats. London abounded with little spots like this—the modern city had grown up around them, but here something of the atmosphere of old London lingered.

No one was in sight. The doors of several garages were closed. Martin glanced at the windows of the other flats, and saw no sign of any one looking out. Most of the curtains were drawn. He walked up a short flight of stone steps to the front door of Number 1. He had taken it for granted that Fraser lived on his own ; he shouldn't have. He might share the flat ; or he might have a servant.

Martin rang the bell ; there was no answer. He rang twice again, with no response. While waiting, he studied the lock of the door, a straightforward Yale. He didn't want to force it, so he turned his attention to a small window at one side. The latch wasn't fastened. He prised the window up an inch with a stout knife, then put his fingers in the gap and thrust the window wide. There was a sharp squeak ; that was all.

He looked round again. His luck was in—there were few places in London so secluded as this.

He climbed in and closed the window, then stood to

one side, looking out. If he had been seen, someone would
almost certainly appear: no one did. There was an outside
chance that someone had seen him and immediately telephoned the police; but if he took no chances he would get
nowhere.

He looked round.

He was in a small passage, with two doors leading from it,
both standing ajar. He looked into one room, a kitchenette,
with another door leading to a bathroom; nothing to interest
him there. He went into the other room. This was long
and narrow, with a door in the far corner. Obviously
Fraser used this as living-cum-dining-room. A small
dining-table was at one end, with a chair at each side.
Table and chairs looked old—dark, oiled oak. Everything
in the room gave the impression of being of good quality.
Bookshelves lined two corners, there were hide arm-chairs
and two saddlebacks. The polished floor had several skin
rugs; and there were the heads of animals on the walls.
One was a lion. Two guns, crossed, were over the big, old-
fashioned fire-place.

In one corner, placed slantwise, was a flat-topped pedestal
desk; the only really modern piece in the room. It was of
walnut, highly polished, and spoke of money. Blotting-pad,
silver ink-stand, and a telephone were on it; nothing else.

On the mantelpiece were two photographs; one of an
elderly woman, the other of Rhoda Grenfell. It was a good
picture. Martin studied it. He hadn't a lot of time, but
years of self-discipline prevented him from hurrying too
much at first. He liked to start slowly. The girl looked
older than she was in real life—more mature was perhaps the
right expression. Every one agreed that she was no fool;
certainly she didn't look it here.

Martin went to the window, which overlooked the mews.
The court was still empty. If the police had been called,
they would have been here by now; so the chance had been
justified. He turned to the desk. He had no zest for forcing
it, this was much more Richard's job than his. He sat down
on a comfortable chair, and pulled at the middle drawer. It
wasn't locked. He opened it and also opened the others;
only one, the bottom drawer on the right, was locked;
and probably everything that really mattered was in there.

He wasn't after valuables but facts about Fraser. He emptied the middle drawer, glancing at all the papers; they told him little. He opened another, and went through that, quite thoroughly. One thing held his interest: a scrap-book. It had photographs and newspaper cuttings of South Africa, Australia, and Brazil. Fraser didn't appear in any of them; nor did the name Fraser appear in any of the cuttings. One name was recurring: Reginald Farraday.

Farraday had a reputation as a hunter and explorer. No hint of his age or appearance was given in any of the cuttings. He was called English or British in several of them. Most of the cuttings were odd-shaped; most told of an expedition he was planning or one he had finished, with the results of it. Martin studied the mutilations; a piece appeared to have been cut out of all of them—and he fancied that in each case the missing part was a photograph.

He began to take it for granted that Reginald Farraday and Reginald Fraser were one and the same man, and warned himself that he could easily make a mistake.

When he glanced at his watch it was half-past eleven; he had been here for half an hour, and hadn't more than half an hour left. He put the scrap-book aside and went through two more drawers. He found a record of three bank accounts, in the name of Fraser—one a deposit account —and of Government bonds. Fraser could call on fifteen thousand pounds any time he liked.

He opened the last drawer.

In an envelope, clipped together, were more Press cuttings. They looked identical at first glance, and had the same head-line, the same sketch of stars, and a planet. Martin's eyes brightened.

THE WEEK IN THE STARS
LENA FORETELLS THE FUTURE

Lena? Hilda Kennedy? The cuttings weren't from the *Sunday Clarion*, they were yellowed as with age. Co-incidence?

He picked up another envelope, but before opening it, heard footsteps approaching the flat.

13

EAVESDROPPING

MARTIN put the papers back in the drawer and closed it. The footsteps stopped. He stood up and went to the door in the corner; there was a bedroom beyond. He stepped inside, half-expecting to hear the front-door bell ring. The caller wasn't a man, the footsteps were too light; so Fraser wasn't back yet.

No bell rang.

He heard other sounds, then the slamming of the door and footsteps in the hall. He stood close to the door of the bedroom, peering through the crack by the hinges. The other door opened, and a girl called:

" Reggie ! "

There was a moment's pause before she came in sight, but Martin didn't need any more identification. Rhoda Grenfell stormed in, looked round exasperatedly at finding the room empty, and called again:

" Reggie ! "

She disappeared; Martin could imagine her looking in the kitchen and bathroom. It wouldn't be long before she came in here. There was a window; he would have just time to climb out. He threw the chance away, crossed to a wardrobe and got inside; the door wouldn't close properly, so he held it. Clothes smothered him, and something soft caught against his nose; he felt an almost irresistible temptation to sneeze. He fought it back, pressing his forefinger against his upper-lip.

" Reggie ! " The girl was much nearer.

He heard her go out without closing the door, opened the door of the wardrobe wider, and took his finger away from his lip. The sneeze caught up with him. He repressed it, but couldn't muffle all sound. He stood rigid, expecting her to come rushing in.

She didn't.

He went to the half-open door and peered cautiously through the crack again into the big room. Rhoda was sitting in an arm-chair, profile towards him, opening her hand-bag. She took out cigarettes, lit one, and leaned her head on the back of the chair and closed her eyes. Again, he was impressed by her look of maturity. He fingered his pipe, but kept it in his pocket.

If Barbara did her job as well as he expected, Fraser would not be back for at least half an hour, and the girl was obviously going to wait for him. Martin moved from the door and sat down in a large arm-chair: Fraser's slippers were on the floor just in front of it. He fought back the desire to smoke, and kept fidgeting, but was careful not to make any noise. Now and again the girl stirred. Each time he prepared to get up, but relaxed when he realised she was only shifting her position. Minutes seemed to crawl.

After about a quarter of an hour the girl stood up. Martin got to his feet and hurried to the door; he didn't think there was much chance that she would come in here again. He could see her without being seen. She went to the desk and sat down; now she faced the door, and might catch sight of any movement. He stood rigid.

She had taken a pencil out of her bag and was writing swiftly; seemed to lose herself in what she was doing. Suddenly her head jerked up and she looked towards the window. Then she sprang to her feet and hurried towards the door, and for the first time Martin heard someone coming. The door opened and the girl left it open. A moment later Martin heard:

" Reggie ! "

" Hallo, my sweet." So Fraser was back a little before his time. " What are you doing here ? "

" Hurry, I have to talk to you."

" Hurrying." Fraser sounded cheerful.

There were footsteps and the sound of a closing door, then the couple came in. Fraser's arm was round the girl's waist, but she didn't give the impression that she had come for a romantic interlude. She kept her body stiff. Fraser kissed her cheek lightly, and she said:

" Don't, Reggie ! This is—important."

" Love's important."

" Darling, I know." She was trying to humour him and at the same time impress him with a sense of urgency. " But I can't stay long, I've been here ages already." She didn't ask where he had been. " I must go away."

Fraser said slowly, " Go *away* ? "

" It's no use. I must."

" Over my dead body," said Fraser. There was a new note in his voice, suggesting that this was an old bone of contention.

Martin stood away from the door, and could neither see nor be seen.

" Please, Reggie." Rhoda's voice had an edge to it. " I can't help it. I've seen—— "

" Hilda."

" I wish I knew why you hate Hilda! "

" Oh, I don't hate her," said Fraser. " I simply think she's a parasite living on fools, and I hate to think of you being a fool, and I hate to think of her blood-sucking from you. Did I ever tell you that I love you ? "

" *Please*, Reggie! "

" You probably think it's odd, but I find it important," Fraser said. " Well, go on. You've seen Hilda again, and she's given you a dire warning. Danger threatens "—he lowered his voice to sepulchral depths, and probably struck an attitude—" and the only way you can escape it is to fly. Right ? "

" Yes."

" Did you ever pause to think that—— "

" Reggie," said Rhoda quietly, " I've paused to think a great deal about a lot of things. Hilda told me that Mother was in danger and said that she ought to leave London. Mother stayed. You know what happened."

" Oh, yes. I also wonder how Hilda Kennedy knew about this danger. Don't tell me that she read it in the stars. I'm an ingenuous young man, but not as ingenuous as that."

" She *does* read the stars."

" If she knew anything was coming to your mother, she didn't find out from the stars," said Fraser heavily.

" You just don't believe it, and nothing will change you." Rhoda was angry. " I've proved time and time again that she really does know what's going to happen. So have others. Why, I've given you proof. I don't think Hilda knows anything about why it happened or who did it—— "

" Stars let her down," said Fraser.

Rhoda exclaimed, " Oh, you're impossible! If you can't be serious, leave me alone."

" You did come to see me," Fraser reminded her.

" I wanted to tell you that I was going. I can't stay any longer. I—Reggie, I'm frightened. Can't you see that? I'm afraid of what might happen to me if I stay in London. If you won't be reasonable, I can't help it. I don't want you to tell anyone—— "

" Is that Hilda's condition? "

" No, she—— " began Rhoda, and hesitated.

Fraser laughed, on a low-pitched, bitter note.

" Oh, no, Hilda didn't tell you to disappear, leaving no trace, did she? Rhoda, when are you going to grow up over this business? Hilda's a menace. Just now, you're a suspect for your mother's murder—— "

" Reggie! "

" Obviously you are." Fraser sounded dogged. " I can't help it if you blink at facts. You're a suspect. If you run away you'll be suspected more strongly. The police will search for you, and probably put a call out. If they don't find you pretty quickly, they'll ask the newspapers to help, and you'll be spread over all the front pages. Perhaps you'd like that."

" It wouldn't matter. *I'd* be safe."

" Oh, yes," said Fraser scornfully. " You'd be as safe as a mouse in a trap. You'd tell Hilda where you were going, of course, and then she'd read the stars and tell someone else. You wouldn't live long. I'll tell you another thing, Rhoda— you'd be murdered, but it would look like suicide. Next, the police would find your body, would decide that you'd killed yourself because you'd killed your mother. *Very* nice. Only I won't allow it to happen."

" You can't keep me here! "

There was a pause; a long one. Martin fought against the temptation to go and look at them. He could imagine them standing face to face, the girl's eyes blazing, Fraser's lips set obstinately. They would make a handsome couple. Martin actually moved, but didn't try to look into the big room. There was tension there, and it managed to pass itself on to him.

Rhoda broke it.

"I came to tell you I'm going away."

Fraser didn't answer.

"If I could rely on you, I'd tell you where, but I can't rely on you. I'll write and tell you where I am—later."

"Nice of you," said Fraser thinly.

"And don't sneer! I hate you when you sneer."

"Oddly enough, I love you all the time," said Fraser. "Now, be sensible for once. Hilda's phoney. All astrologers are. I tell you that you'll be in grave danger if you do what she says. You ought to tell Fane about this." His voice rose. "Yes, that's it. Go and tell Fane. You're trusting enough where he's concerned. Take his advice."

"I'm not going to ask anyone's advice. I know what I'm going to do."

"I see," said Fraser heavily.

There was another pause; not so long, and with less tension. Martin waited, finding himself smiling faintly. Then Rhoda spoke with an inflection in her voice which didn't surprise him.

"Reggie, I hate quarrelling like this. I'm sure you're wrong about Hilda. If mother had taken her advice she would be alive now. Someone wants us both dead. I don't know who it is, and I'm—terrified. After what happened to Mother, I've hardly been able to think. I saw the police, and it was hateful—all I could think about was getting away. I'd told myself that I would do what you wanted, and that with Prince helping me it would be all right, but when I saw Hilda again—— "

"I know," said Fraser quietly. "Rhoda, listen to me—and look at me."

There was a pause.

"You trust Hilda Kennedy. Why not trust me, for a change? I saw Fane this morning. He's sound, if ever a man is, and—— "

"There you are," said Rhoda flatly. "A few hours ago you told me I was a fool for going to see him, that I ought to leave everything to the police. Now you're all for him. You change from minute to minute, you're just not reliable over this. I *must* go. I'm sorry. When it's all over we'll be able to live normally again."

Fraser said abruptly, "Oh, no."

" What do you mean ? "

Fraser didn't speak, but started to pace the room. Martin heard his footsteps, and flattened himself against the door as they drew nearer. He needn't have worried : Fraser turned back and walked across the room again. Now there was tension ; the pause was prolonged, he could imagine the girl standing and watching Fraser as he prowled.

" What do you *mean* ? " she demanded with a catch in her voice.

" Just this." Fraser's tone was abrupt. " If you can be crazy enough to do what Hilda Kennedy advises, instead of being advised by me, I'm through. Through, completely. It would mean that I'd never be sure of you. At any time you might dash off on some crazy errand that Hilda, or some other star-gazer, persuaded you was necessary. If you go now, that'll be that. Make up your mind."

The girl didn't speak.

Fraser said more warmly, " Rhoda, I hate saying it. If I weren't so sure you're wrong, I wouldn't. But you're not to do what Hilda Kennedy tells you. I'm sure it would be fatal. I can't let you do it."

Another pause followed.

" I see," said Rhoda heavily. " I didn't think it would come to this, I thought you meant what you said about— loving me. I'm going, Reggie. So we may as well resign ourselves to it."

" Rhoda—— "

" I'm going," she said, with a tone of finality which even Fraser couldn't question. " Hilda's genuine. She's been a good friend to me, and she's never failed me, her advice has always been sound. If you weren't sceptical, you'd feel the same way as I do. Why *don't* you believe ? I've given you proof enough, any reasonable man would agree that she's been right, that she has some unaccountable gift. If she made a fortune out of it I could understand you doubting her, but she doesn't, she—— "

" How do you know ? " flashed Fraser. " She pays a fortune in rent for that flat. Where does she get her money from ? "

" Oh, you're impossible ! "

Martin heard a flurry of movement, and could picture the

girl hurrying towards the door; another flurry, and he knew that Fraser was going after her. He couldn't resist any longer, but went to the door. They were near the other door, Fraser holding her by the shoulders, Rhoda struggling to free herself. She butted his face with the back of her head, but he saw it coming, and escaped the full force of the blow. Then he spun her round. It was a swift, powerful movement; she was quite helpless against it. For a moment they were face to face; then Fraser struck her on the chin.

It wasn't a powerful blow; at least, it didn't look powerful, but it was expert. The girl crumpled up, knees bending. Fraser saved her from falling, then lifted her and carried her to a chair. He lowered her gently and stood back, looking down at her. Abruptly, he went down on one knee and took her limp hand, pressed it to his lips, and held it tightly. He let it go slowly, reluctantly.

Her head lolled against the back of the chair.

Fraser stood up.

" Sorry," he said, in a curt, hurt voice. " Had to, darling. I can't let you be fooled by that old witch. But how am I going to keep you away from her? Where can I take you? I can't keep you here."

He paused.

Martin waited until he had recovered from the shock of what had happened, and then opened the door wide and stood in the doorway.

14 SANCTUARY

FRASER stood looking down at Rhoda, hand at his head, forehead wrinkled. His lips were curved wryly. He didn't see Martin at once. He took out cigarettes, put one to his lips, and lit it slowly. The girl looked relaxed, and he had placed her in a graceful posture; it would be difficult to put Rhoda Grenfell into any other. Her head lolled naturally against the back of the chair, and her hair swept off her forehead.

" Quite a problem, isn't it ? " asked Martin.

Fraser started, but didn't turn round quickly. He steeled himself, backed a pace, then turned his head. Relief drove the anxiety out of his eyes; they were fine eyes. The more Martin saw of Fraser, the more he liked his looks and general manner.

"Hallo," said Fraser. "You get about."

"It's how I earn my bread."

"The proper thing is to ask you what the hell you're doing in my flat."

"And you'd hate not to do the proper thing," said Martin. He grinned. "I opened a window and climbed in."

"So I'm your bad man."

"You could be," Martin said, and stopped grinning. "I don't have to ask what you're doing with Rhoda. I heard everything. Why don't you let her run away?"

"So it's your advice, too."

"I'm just seeking motives."

"You detectives must lead a hard life," said Fraser flippantly; facetiousness came easily to him, even now. "You have to turn everything you hear inside out before you can decide whether to believe it. Try believing what you heard me tell Rhoda. It's true."

"It could be," said Martin. "Where's it going to get you?"

"Police?" hazarded Fraser. "Common assault is the technical term, I believe. Or can you suggest a nice little spot where I could take her? A sanctuary. After all, you private dicks have all kinds of secret weapons up your sleeves, haven't you? An emergency like this must be chicken feed. Yes? No?"

He stubbed out his cigarette; he hadn't drawn at it three times.

"Yes," said Martin.

Fraser took out another cigarette and lit it. There was no other sound in the room, and Rhoda was still unconscious; she wasn't likely to stay that way much longer.

"Where?" The word was barked.

"My people's place, in Dorset."

"Your *family*? You mean, *Jonathan* Fane's house."

Martin nodded.

"Damn it," exploded Fraser, "he writes this kind of thing, he doesn't live it!"

"I'd as lief talk to him about it as anyone," said Martin. "He'll play, too. My mother will protest vigorously, but won't close the door. It's a nice house, good food and all that kind of thing. It might be possible to persuade Rhoda to stay there and like it. After all, you'd both have your own way. She wouldn't be in Hilda Kennedy's hands, and she would be out of London. Think she's genuinely frightened?"

"If you were anyone else I'd say don't be a fool." Fraser smoked the second cigarette more naturally. "Why ask? Do you think she could put up an act like that?"

"I'm trying to find out," said Martin.

"Let's try later." Fraser glanced at the girl again; she stirred a little. "Come to think, it's going to be a hell of a job to make her sit quiet in a car while we take her to Dorset. From this moment on, my name will be mud."

"Good," said Martin warmly.

"Thanks."

"I'll take her," said Martin. "You stay here. I'll tell her that I came unexpectedly, that you had to go out and left me to wait in another room, and I found her. Something she'll believe, anyhow."

"I must say," said Fraser with great deliberation, "that you're not bad. I'll play, if you will. And if she will."

"Go and make sure that no one's outside, will you? And if you can drive a Buick, bring the one from the next corner into the mews."

"Keys, please," said Fraser.

Martin handed them over, and Fraser went off.

The girl stirred again and her lips moved, but she didn't open her eyes. Martin lifted her bodily; she was surprisingly light. Fraser soon drove into the mews, and Martin carried the girl down the steps and lifted her into his car. He took the wheel, and flicked a card across to Fraser, one with the Nairn Lodge address. Fraser nodded. Martin nosed the car out of the mews, and looked right and left. He didn't think that he had been followed, or that the flat was watched. He drove by back streets to his flat. By the time he reached it, the girl was sitting up and looking dazedly about her. She didn't protest when he took her arm, helped her out and led her up the stairs; her footsteps flagged. He went in cautiously, but there was nothing to fear. He led her to a large arm-chair, waited until she sat down, and then lifted the telephone. She was much better; there was a look of intelligent understanding in her eyes as she watched him.

He dialled the office, and Jessica answered.

" Oh, just a minute, sir, I'll ring her." Martin heard her call, " It's Mr. Martin," and then Barbara spoke.

" Hallo, Scoop."

" How did it go ? " asked Martin.

" I've been waiting to hear from you," said Barbara ruefully. " He was like a cat on hot bricks, and wouldn't stay for long. I tried everything I could, but—— "

" It's all right. I'm going down to Dorset, and taking Rhoda Grenfell with me."

Barbara didn't speak. Rhoda sat up in her chair, and began to frown.

" I think it'll be better and safer to get her out of town, and I'd like to have a talk with the Maestro on this case," said Martin. " Will you hold the fort ? "

" Of course, darling. What does she say about it ? "

Martin laughed. " She doesn't know, yet. Well, hardly."

" I'm not sure that I like you much when you're obscure," said Barbara. " But if it will help, be mysterious. Ring me as soon as you're home, won't you ? "

" The very moment," said Martin.

He rang off, looking down at Rhoda, but thinking of Barbara. She would have told him if there had been any other development; there were so many blanks. With Rhoda at home, he might get a clearer story out of her, but he doubted whether he would discover why Fraser had clippings of an astrologer's prophecies in his drawer. He could shut that out of his mind, for the time being; if Fraser were genuine he would be helpful from now on—and informative.

Rhoda said slowly, " If this is Reggie's idea—— "

Martin was ready for that one.

" Oh, but it isn't. Mine entirely. I called to see him, he left me in the flat while he went out for ten minutes, and one of the rooms was locked. I found you there. Not surprising, as I'd seen you come." He put his head on one side as he spoke. " You'll like my people and, with luck, they'll like you. And you'll be out of danger for the time being, at least."

" So you think I am in danger."

" I'm sure you think so. This should give you some peace of mind."

" All right," she said. " I'll come—on one condition."

" Yes ? "

" You're not working for Reggie as well, are you ? "

Martin chuckled. " One at a time is best."

" Is that true ? "

" He's not a client of mine, and isn't likely to be," said Martin firmly. " Come with me and relax. My brother's down there already, so it'll be a family party."

She nodded, almost as if pleased.

" I'll get you a drink," said Martin. He went to the cocktail cabinet and mixed a whisky-and-soda. " This'll do you good. Then I have to go out for twenty minutes—you can rest. That crack over the head wasn't fun, was it ? "

" That he could do it to *me*—— "

" Lovers' quarrel ? " asked Martin lightly.

She didn't answer.

He picked up the 'phone and called King's, a small inquiry agency, which sometimes worked with him. It wasn't difficult to arrange what he wanted—for a man to come here and follow them to Dorset.

He waited until he saw the man, and then hurried round to the office.

Barbara was on the telephone, and rang off quickly.

" A lost dog inquiry," she said lightly. " Have you stopped being mysterious ? "

" Partly." He told her what had happened.

She made no comment, but obviously approved of the Dorset move. Fraser had been very edgy, she hadn't learned much more from him.

He left hurriedly, and when he got back to the flat, Rhoda was standing up and looking at herself in the mirror. She had made up and had shaken off the effect of the blow. She looked young and supremely attractive.

The King's Agency man was still outside, ready to follow.

They lunched on the road. Martin knew the agency car, but the driver—one of the King partners—showed no sign of recognition, although they sat in the same dining-room. After that Martin let the Buick go all out. The road was good, and there was little traffic. The girl made an occasional comment, but seemed content to sit back and watch the passing countryside.

It was still bleak from the hand of late winter. Trees were etched against a cold blue sky. The grass had a radiant greenness, and along part of the road firs stood dark in their perpetual cloak of green.

They left the tree-clad country and drove through the rolling fields of Hampshire, reaching wooded stretches again in Dorset. Four and a half hours after leaving London, Martin turned the car into the gates of Nairn Lodge. This was a graceful Georgian building, standing in several acres of well-kept grounds. Lawns on either side of the drive were trim and neat. Flower-beds were freshly turned, and in some of them wallflower plants looked flourishing and bushy. He slowed down up the steep drive, and suddenly the girl exclaimed:

"Look!" There was alarm in her voice.

Martin's foot went on the brake. "What is it?"

"I saw—a man. There, among the trees. He's—— "

The man appeared again, a man clad in white but with a coal-black face. Martin relaxed and chuckled. The girl stared at the black man, as if at a freak. The man was going to a small shed, nearly hidden by trees: a summer-house. Martin waved; and the black face nearly split in two, to show a set of gleaming white teeth. Words came across the still, chilly air:

"Glad see yo', Massa Martin!"

"Who is it?" Rhoda demanded faintly.

"Sampson. Our butler," explained Martin. "Call him anything, he's man of all work. My father brought him over from Jamaica, years ago, and he's a fixture. You'll like Sampson. If you don't, there's something wrong with you."

Rhoda didn't speak.

The car pulled up outside the house. As the engine

was turned off a different sound reached their ears—the ceaseless tap-tap-tap of a typewriter. Martin glanced smilingly up at an open window. Then he helped Rhoda out, and as he did so, the door opened and a tall, well-dressed woman appeared. She had iron-grey hair, a broad face, and fresh complexion. She wasn't beautiful, but there was something attractive about her appearance, and her smile was wide as she greeted Martin.

"Hallo, Scoop, it's good to see you, but *why* didn't you say you were coming?"

"The unexpected pleasure's best," said Martin, and kissed her cheek. "You're still wearing well, sweetheart!"

"No blarney from you," said Evelyn Fane. "I've had enough from Richard to last me for weeks." She laughed, as she looked at Rhoda and waited for Martin to introduce the girl. When she heard the name Grenfell she frowned and tightened her lips; that was soon over, and she smiled again, but the smile lacked warmth. "How are you?"

"How d'you do?" said Rhoda. "And please don't blame me, it was your son's idea."

"Blame? I don't understand you." Evelyn Fane put a hand on Martin's arm. "You'll want some tea, I'll tell Sampson to get some as soon as he's in. Look after Miss Grenfell, Martin, won't you? I'll be down in a few minutes." She went towards a flight of wide stairs, which led off a delightfully furnished hall carpeted from wall to wall. Oil paintings, all landscapes, hung on the walls; there was an atmosphere of well-being and of discernment here.

Rhoda said, "I don't think it was a good idea, after all."

"Oh, don't worry about Mother. I warned you." Martin led the girl into a small room, a bright room of primrose yellow and apple green; obviously a woman's room. Slender daffodils stood in tall vases on a small book-case. Tapestry work, a threaded needle still in it, lay on a table by the side of an arm-chair turned so that whoever sat there could get a good light from the window. "Come and sit down," said Martin. "How's the head?"

"Aching a bit. Nothing to worry about." But Rhoda sat down as if she were in some pain, she looked pale and tired from the journey. "I've been thinking as we came down in the car. How can I be *sure* I'm safe here? How can we be sure that the man who was escorting us would see any one else following us? How would he know?"

"He's good at the job. It's easy to pick out a car which is following another. In any case, if you'd gone somewhere else, how could you have been sure that you weren't being followed?"

Rhoda had no answer.

"We'll have time to dig deep while you're here," said Martin. "I shall probably go back to-night, but you'll be all right. Sampson's worth a couple of men by himself. Now—my father will be down in a minute, that's what my mother went upstairs for. Don't be surprised if he seems a bit vague. It will be partly because he's just stopped working, he was busy on that fantastic typewriter of his. It will be partly because he isn't sure of the situation yet, and won't have made up his mind whether he wants to square Mother or not. And it will be partly"—Martin grinned—"mostly, I should say, just because he's Jonathan Fane. He'll want to take your measure before he shows anything of his real self, but—get him on your side, Rhoda."

She didn't speak.

"It matters," Martin said. "It's one of the reasons why I brought you down here. I think they're coming."

He turned to the door. Footsteps sounded outside, and there was a murmur of voices. Rhoda stood up as the door opened, and Evelyn Fane came in, followed by her husband.

The door had hardly closed on them when the telephone bell rang.

15 THE FANE FAMILY

THE bell rang again.

"Oh, drat the thing!" exclaimed Evelyn Fane. "I was a fool ever to have one in here If you weren't too lazy to walk to the other room, we shouldn't be pestered by it every time I'm sitting back and relaxing." She dropped into an arm-chair.

Jonathan Fane looked at her with dull, uninspiring eyes.

" Sorry, darling.   If you want to rest—— "

" You know perfectly well what I mean," snapped Evelyn.   " Don't try to be funny."

Martin was grinning, his father's face remained blank, Evelyn Fane looked angry.   Rhoda, turning from one to the other and seeing the Fane family together for the first time, probably felt that she couldn't cope.   She sat down.

" Well, who's going to answer it ? " demanded Evelyn. " I suppose you'll leave it to me, as you leave everything else in this house.   It's probably someone who wants to borrow money."

" I'll take it," said Fane.   " It may be about the Church Fête."   He moved towards the telephone, lifted the receiver, waited, and said, " Jonathan Fane here. . . . Yes, he is, hold on, please."

He held the telephone out to Martin, who went across and took it, while watching his mother eyeing Rhoda.   He had come to respect his mother's judgment on other people ; they sometimes seemed waspish, but were usually on the mark.

" Hallo," he said.

" King here," said a man at the other end of the line. " You were followed by a big Humber.   Chauffeur driven, woman at the back.   The chauffeur did a good job, I wasn't sure until the last minute."

Martin said, " Oh, thanks.   I'll be seeing you."

He rang off, still smiling, hiding the fact that the news was disquieting.   King wouldn't make a mistake.

His father was shaking hands with Rhoda ; that was characteristic of Jonathan Fane ; he had taken to the girl at first sight.   He wasn't as reliable in quick character judgment as his wife, who seemed to be watching Rhoda warily.

Evelyn stood up suddenly, unexpectedly.

" I know you two want to talk, and Miss Grenfell looks tired.   I think we'll go in the other room and have a cup of tea together."

Good sign, thought Martin.

" My sweet, I shouldn't dream of turning you out," said Jonathan.   " We'll go up to the study.   Sampson can bring us some tea up there." He beamed at Rhoda, and led the way to the door.

There was just room on the stairs for the men to walk side by side. Martin was an inch or two taller than his father, with much the same build. Jonathan Fane was plump without being fat, full-faced, good-looking when one looked at him full face, but needing more of a chin and less of an incipient jowl to make his profile worth a second glance. Iron-grey hair, inclined to wave, grew well back on his forehead ; he showed no sign of a bald patch. He wore a pair of grey flannel trousers and an old jacket and a sports shirt. As he reached the head of the stairs he loosened his tie, which had been knotted out of deference to his wife rather than to impress Rhoda. He walked with a slight limp, and lit a cigarette as he entered a book-lined study, large enough to look spacious and small enough for comfort. Two book-cases, taking up most of one wall, were filled with books he had written ; hundreds of them. Two shelves were given to books about the Prince, the fabulous character who had given the agency its name. All were in their original gaudy and gory jackets.

The furniture was plain and well polished. A standard typewriter stood on a huge desk, with piles of paper on either side of it ; the machine was empty, which meant that although he must have heard the car draw up, Fane had finished the page he was writing before taking any notice. On the right of the typewriter was a big ash-tray, filled with cigarette-butts ; on the left a carved Kashmir box, containing a hundred or so cigarettes. The study was filled with the haze and smell of tobacco smoke, although it was chilly and two windows were open.

Fane went to a chair behind the desk and sat down, as Martin put in a call to the office ; it would take some time to come through.

"Who called you ? " Fane asked, and his grey eyes were smiling, the right screwed up slightly, to keep out the smoke which crept beneath his thick horn-rimmed glasses. "It was a local call, and the village doesn't know you're here. Or does it ? "

"The windows were all lined with prying eyes," said Martin. "But the call was from King. I asked him to tail me. He says we were followed by a chauffeur-driven Humber with a woman passenger. It doesn't sound deadly."

" Wise precaution," said Fane, and waited for Martin to talk. He would be full of questions when he felt the moment ripe.

Martin talked freely. There was a bond between father and son, much stronger than a simple blood-tie. They had the same outlook, often saw the same slant, shared the same philosophy. Richard was cast much more in his mother's mould.

Fane chain-smoked as he listened, nodded occasionally, actually made two pencilled notes. The London call came, Martin re-assured Barbara, then finished his story.

" And that's it," he said at last. " I couldn't think of anywhere else to take her at the moment. If necessary, we can find somewhere from here."

" Do you want the police to hunt for her ? "

Martin shrugged. " If I hadn't taken her away she'd have gone somewhere."

" She looks as if she knows her own mind," said Fane. " She's all right, I should say, and I fancy your mother thinks so, too. What's Reginald Fraser like ? "

" Doubtful, with a bias on the favourable side."

" Hmm," said Fane, and lit another cigarette. " First things first. The police will soon find out that she's dis-appeared. Know what I'd do, if I were you ? "

Martin shook his head ; he guessed, but let the older man make the point.

" Tell Scotland Yard. Not young Wimple—Chief In-spector Oakes, or even Superintendent Kelby. Take them into your confidence. I think you're right, and Wimple was sent on a special mission to see you. If you put some cards on the table, they'll be happier and will listen to reason. You won't tell Rhoda what you've done, of course."

Martin shook his head.

" But you'll do it ? "

" Yes."

" Good ! Apart from that, you haven't a lot to go on yet." Fane was thoughtful. " No idea at all what's behind it, obviously. High-pressuring Hilda Kennedy was the right thing, but obviously she's tough. Always difficult to deal with these people who are a bit odd, and I've heard that she really takes her business seriously, no tongue in the cheek. Oddest thing you've found was that bunch of clippings that Fraser had. Not Hilda Kennedy's, you say."

"Not under her name, anyhow. The name was 'Lena '."

"Good thing to check if any one in the star-gazing world ever heard of her," said Fane. "Grenfell, now—I wonder what his angle is. Make anything of it yourself?"

Martin stretched out his legs—and then heard a faint sound at the door. He glanced round; it was opening slowly. He didn't show that he had noticed it, but shook his head and said firmly:

"None."

"Just what I expected," boomed Richard, and came in breezily. "Hallo, Scoop! Don't be ashamed of not having a single idea in your head, all the family can't be blessed."

He wore an old sports jacket and grey flannel trousers, both of which looked as if they had just been freshly pressed. His eyes were still a little bloodshot, but he looked much better than he had that morning. He dropped into a hide arm-chair and pushed his fingers through his wavy hair. "Now *I'm* full of ideas."

"You were last night," said Jonathan Fane dryly.

"Take it easy. Look at the results I nearly got. It's not every one who gets a front stall at a murder." The flippancy was on his lips but not in his eyes. "Hell of a business. No farther on, Scoop? I saw the luscious Rhoda out of the window, you must have exerted all your personal magnetism to get her here."

"We'll need yours to keep her," retorted Martin. "Where were we? Oh, yes, ideas." No one interrupted, and he took his time. "It started with Rhoda coming to us with half a story, and Hilda Kennedy apparently approving. Just to get us interested. Then came Grenfell, with a story which seems to stand up—I can't see any weakness in it, anyhow. Then came violence—to try to frighten us off, I fancy. Then the murder, and after that——"

"Silence," said Richard in a deep voice.

"They haven't had a lot of time to do anything else," said

Fane. " No evidence yet that they want to do anything else, is there ? "

" Except that Rhoda's frightened," Martin reminded him.

Fane nodded. " The immediate worry is to keep Rhoda here and make sure we don't have trouble," he said. " Your mother wouldn't take kindly to that. She's worried enough about Richard ; if she knew everything, she'd be terrified. I can see trouble looming up if the police learn that Richard was at the scene of the murder," he added, with solemn understatement.

Richard gave a mock shudder. " I feel the dead hand of suspicion already."

" That won't do any harm if it will keep you quiet for a bit. I wonder what's happened to that tea."

Fane stood up quickly—and as he did so, Evelyn Fane's voice sounded from downstairs. The brothers had often noticed the way in which both parents seemed to think of the same thing at the same time.

" Jon ! " called Evelyn.

" Hallo ? "

" Where *is* Sampson ? I thought you said he wouldn't be many minutes."

" Wondering myself," said Fane, from the landing. His wife was at the foot of the stairs, and the brothers were standing near the window, looking out. They saw the big black car coming along the narrow road which led to Nairn Lodge ; only Martin was really affected, for the car was a Humber. Richard was whistling softly, his mother was calling up the stairs, words he couldn't clearly catch.

The Humber turned into the drive, the engine running smoothly. Martin saw the chauffeur at the wheel, but couldn't see the woman passenger.

He did see the man standing behind a bush near the drive : a man with his right hand raised, and a gun in it pointing towards the car.

.   .   .   .   .

Martin roared, " Look out ! " as he flung himself towards the open window, pushed it up and leaned out. " Look out, there ! " He saw the gunman glance round, and the chauffeur turn towards the house, startled. The car stopped. The man probably hadn't heard the words.

Richard was just behind Martin, and muttered, " If only we had a gun—— "

Evelyn's voice came sharply, " What's the matter ? "

Martin pushed away from the window, bumped into Richard—and then saw the man behind the bushes shoot. He saw the flashes of flame and heard the sharp roar of the shots, the noise as a bullet hit the metal of the car. He saw the driver slump forward in his seat, and thought that someone in the back of the car also fell.

Richard, white and tense, was staring.

Jonathan Fane stood in the doorway.

Martin said, " Look out ! " He pushed past his father and rushed down the stairs. His mother was half-way up, Rhoda was in the doorway of the morning-room.

" Scoop ! " screamed his mother.

" Won't be long." He pushed past her, jumped the last few stairs, and rushed to the front door. He couldn't see the gunman, and the shooting had stopped ; it was a waste of time. He didn't let that stop him, but raced down the drive, jumped up on to the bank where the gunman had been, and was slowed down by the springy, rain-soaked turf. He went on, peering through bushes and trees.

He caught a glimpse of a man near the hedge which bordered the garden ; the man was forcing his way through. He faced Martin—and Martin saw his gun move. Martin flung himself sideways as the shot roared out. He didn't know what happened to the bullet, but started off again. The man was out of sight now, and as Martin ran on, he heard the staccato beat of a motor-cycle engine.

He slowed down.

There wasn't a chance of catching the man, and none of giving chase, while the Humber blocked the narrow drive. He drew almost level with it and turned towards it, seeing the shiny black body in the gathering dusk. As he reached the gravel of the drive, Richard came running, and his mother and Rhoda were on the porch ; there was no sign of Fane.

He looked at the car.

The chauffeur was slumped over the wheel with blood on

his face. A woman leaned back on the seat, deathly pale, but with her eyes open.

It was Hilda Kennedy.

16   "BRING 'EM ALL"

THE woman's terrified eyes were fixed on Martin, but he glanced away, towards the driver. He opened the nearest door and leaned inside, easing the man's body from the wheel; he felt a dead weight and the sticky drip of blood. He steeled himself to face whatever there was to see.

The bullet had gone through the man's forehead, just above the nose. Because he had fallen forward, the blood had flowed freely. His peaked cap was still stuck to the back of his head. He had a small, wizened face : the face of an oldish man.

Martin rested him against the seat, closed the door, and opened that by the side of the woman. She had stared all the time, but hadn't uttered a word. Now she gulped, began to speak, managed only a few inarticulate sounds, and lapsed into silence. Martin edged in beside her, and asked :

" Were you hit ? "

She shook her head ; it was like the movement of a puppet being jerked by a string. He could see no blood on her, nothing to suggest that she was suffering from more than shock.

" I'll help you out," he said.

She seemed incapable of moving by herself; he had to drag her out. By the time she was on the drive and leaning against him, every one except Fane and Sampson was at the spot. Richard was brisk ; Richard usually kept his head in a real emergency.

" Mother, if you and Rhoda will take her up to the house, we'll move the car a bit." He stood in front of the dead driver ; it was impossible to be sure whether either Evelyn Fane or Rhoda had seen what had happened. Neither of them tried to look beyond Richard, and Martin supported Hilda Kennedy past the bonnet ; then they took her arms, one on each side, and started up the drive towards the house. Martin saw his father's grey head, near the window ; Fane was at the telephone, and turning so that he could see what was going on.

" Lucky Hilda," Richard said.

" Could be. Have you seen Sampson ? "

" Not lately." Richard frowned. " Why—— "

" What's Dad doing ? "

" I don't know, but I'd guess he's talking to the police."

" Nothing more we can do here," said Martin. " Let's look for Sampson."

" The car—— "

Martin exploded, " Damn the car ! "

" I see what you mean."

They moved towards the side of the drive where the little summer-house stood. Fane occasionally used it for work, on really hot days, and kept some of his old manuscripts and stationery there. Presumably he had sent Sampson for something, and Sampson was renowned for being quick when Jonathan Fane gave the word.

The brothers approached from different sides ; it was Martin who first saw a pair of feet.

Then he saw Sampson's head.

He clenched his teeth.

The Negro's hair was crinkly and snowy white, except where there was blood. There was no sign of injury apart from the head. Martin went down on one knee as Richard came in sight. Richard stopped, caught his breath, and watched for what seemed an interminable time. Then he swore ; he seldom swore, it wasn't a Fane habit, they managed to avoid it without seeming priggish. Now Richard let himself go—on what he would do to the man who had attacked Sampson.

They couldn't remember the time when Sampson hadn't served them.

Richard's voice was hoarse when he said, " How is he ? "

Martin was fingering the black man's pulse, while looking at his head.

" Fair," he said, taking off his coat. He put it over the Negro. " I hope to heaven it's true that black skulls are thick. Better leave him here until we can get an ambulance."

Richard took his coat off, and added it to Martin's. " Will you go and ring for an ambulance ? " Martin added. " Bring back blankets—or mother's fur coat. Tell her we'll want hot-water bottles."

Richard nodded, and went off; he broke into a run, and ploughed across a flower-bed which he would usually have avoided as if it were the plague. Martin didn't watch him, but made sure there was nothing else he could do for Sampson; the bleeding had slackened. The blow hadn't been struck within the last five minutes, but probably before Martin had gone up to the study. The assailant had been hiding in or behind the summer-house, and Sampson had been a danger.

There were plenty of footprints. The ground round the summer-house was wet, and there wasn't much grass. A man with small feet had waited and moved about here; the man he had seen had been small: five feet six or seven. So had one of the men whom he had seen on the first night of the affair. Sampson's footsteps showed, too; he'd obviously gone into the summer-house and been attacked on his way out. Then the man had dragged him round to the back, to make sure that he couldn't be seen from the window.

Jonathan Fane had probably been sitting with his back to the window when it had happened; a chance glance outside, and he might have seen.

Martin lit his pipe, heard footsteps, and saw his father walking down the drive. Soon Fane was staring down at his servant. He didn't speak. His face was set, and his eyes were bleak. He lit a cigarette slowly.

" Good thing you didn't move him."

" Think the ambulance will be long ? "

" I'd already sent for one," said Fane, " I could see that the driver would have to be carried away. Through the police, of course. The ambulance, I mean. I mentioned the motor-cycle, too. Heard it." He was drawing heavily at his cigarette. " We'd better get that car shifted, there's room down near the gate. Plenty of room to pass there. Didn't touch the driver much, did you ? "

" No." Martin felt a lump in his throat. " I'm damned sorry, Dad. Didn't think this would bring it right home."

"I'm glad it did." They turned, and met Richard coming down the drive. None of them spoke as they reached the Humber. Martin manœuvred the wheel, touching the dead man all the time, and they eased it down towards the gates, where the drive was wide enough for it to be parked, and let the police cars and other traffic pass. That done, they went back to Sampson.

"No need for us all to stay," said Fane. "Go and see how your mother's getting on."

Martin said, "Right."

"Oh, Scoop."

"Yes?"

"Don't tell her about Sampson. Leave that to me."

"All right."

The brothers walked slowly up the drive; more slowly because Richard obviously found it hard going, and he was breathing heavily when they reached the porch. Martin studied him, thought fleetingly of the girl in Hollywood and of the girl in Fulham. Richard was often unpredictable, but there were times when Martin felt that he could be as sure of Richard's thoughts as he was of his own. They were thinking exactly the same thing: that they hadn't anything to congratulate themselves over.

They went into the hall.

Richard exploded, "And we had to bring this *here*."

"My fault."

"Like hell it's your fault," said Richard. "I'm going out of the foul business."

"People have found us useful."

"Thinking of that chauffeur?"

Martin shrugged, but didn't speak. They went upstairs, and could hear voices coming from one of the spare rooms. Inside, Evelyn Fane and Rhoda were standing and looking down at Hilda Kennedy, who was lying on the bed, fully dressed except for her shoes. They had loosened her clothes, and Evelyn had a glass in her hand; probably brandy. Obviously there was nothing the men could do. Martin nudged his brother, and they went into the study. It was now nearly dark.

"Wonder what the star-gazer wanted here," Richard said, in an easier voice. He went to a cupboard where Fane kept whisky, gin, and soda—and soft drinks. He was a teetotaller; neither of his sons had followed his example. Richard began to pour out, and didn't add much soda. " Think she followed you ? "

" She followed me all right. Whether she was on the way before I was, or whether she discovered that I was bringing Rhoda here, is any one's guess. We'll find out. King warned me we were followed by the Humber. He didn't mention the man on the motor-bike. Could be—— " He paused.

" Fellow came on first and was waiting," said Richard. " Notice any of the speed-fiends pass you on the road ? " He brought the whisky-and-soda over. " Here's to the death of a killer."

They drank.

" Several passed me," said Martin. " Our man probably started to follow, guessed that I was coming down here, and decided to make a reception party—but not for me. That suggests they also knew that Hilda Kennedy was coming this way."

" Who knew *you* were coming ? "

" Fraser." Richard had heard nothing of Fraser; Martin told him, and was still talking when an ambulance turned in at the gates, headlights on. Jonathan Fane, standing in the gloom by the side of the drive, raised a hand to stop it. In the light of headlights and torches Sampson was lifted on to a stretcher and taken to the ambulance. When that moved off, another car turned into the drive. Richard, at the whisky bottle again, said :

" Police."

" Probably. Don't overdo the Scotch."

" No, Solomon." Richard tossed down the first half of his second drink. " Mother's a long time, isn't she ? "

They hadn't heard Evelyn Fane leave Hilda Kennedy's room. They went out, and every one met on the landing. Fane, a C.I.D. Inspector from Dorchester, the nearest town, Evelyn, Rhoda, and the brothers ; and no one said a word. At the foot of the stairs stood one of the plain-clothes men and a servant.

Fane said, " Inspector, you'll have to excuse me for five minutes. Take Inspector Cornley into the study, boys, and outline the story. You'll excuse me too, Miss Grenfell, won't you?" He took his wife's arm. She didn't protest as he led her into the big bedroom which overlooked the drive. He closed the door with a snap, then opened it again and called, "Scoop!"

Martin came to the door.

"Get at the Kennedy woman before the police have a chance," whispered Fane, and closed the door again almost immediately.

His wife stood with her back to the wide windows. The curtains weren't drawn, and the darkness of the night showed against them, with a speckling of stars. A soft wind blew gently in beech-trees which grew near the house. There was quietness. By the drive gates were car lights and the shadowy figures of men, but their voices didn't travel this far.

The room was large and lofty, with a big double bed and heavy mahogany furniture. It had the same charm as the rest of the house; everything matched. Fane went towards his wife, his footsteps muffled by the deep pile of the carpet. He took her hands. She didn't speak. Her eyes were bright, and her full lips were tremulous; in times of stress her lips were always likely to quiver. She looked as if she might cry; or as if she might flare up with wild anger.

Fane said, "You've guessed that Sampson's been hurt, haven't you?"

She nodded.

"I don't think he's hurt badly. Certainly not fatally."

"How on earth do you *know*?" Evelyn burst out. "You're only saying that to comfort me. I won't be smarmed over." Her eyes blazed, and she pulled herself free. "I can't stand this beastly business any longer. It's bad enough that you have to write about crime, without the boys *stinking* with it. They've got to stop. It won't go on —I'll make them stop somehow. *You* must make them stop. If it weren't for your money and the fact that they know you're behind them, they would have given it up ages ago. I—— "

"We can talk about that later," said Fane. "Just now—— "

" Later ! " cried Evelyn scornfully. " Later, later, later !
That's what you always say.   I won't wait any longer, someone has to make a decision.   Richard comes home looking
as if he were at death's door, Martin goes rushing after a
man with a gun and brings a whore to our home, now this
woman is here, the police are trampling all over the house,
heaven knows when it will end.   But *I* know.   This is the
last time, the very last time that it ever happens."

" All right," said Fane gently.   " But Richard's really in a
bad spot, my sweet.   I didn't tell you everything.   Richard
could become a suspect.   Murder.   Don't put any added
strain on him or on Scoop just now.   Let's get this over."

His wife whispered, " *What ?* "

" It'll be all right, but it's nerve-racking for them," Fane
said.   " If you—— "

His wife seemed to fall forward, and his arms went round
her.   They stood together for several minutes, and then he
eased her gently away from him.   She moved quickly, swung
to the dressing-table, and spoke in a muffled voice.

" I'll be all right.   You go and see the others.   They'll
need you."

" I'll be back soon," said Fane.

He went out, closing the door softly.   No one was on
the spacious landing, but a C.I.D. man stood at the foot of
the stairs, and noticed Fane.   Fane looked out of the landing
window and saw the police busy in the light of torches, near
the Humber; they were taking photographs; flashes lit up
the grounds.

Martin was coming along the passage from the spare room.
Fane waited.

" I can't get any sense out of Hilda," Martin said.   " I
don't think she'll talk to any one to-night.   We'd better
make sure that she sees a doctor, too—can you fix it with
Tucker ?   Better he than a police-surgeon."

" Nip downstairs and telephone Tuck from the drawing-
room," said Fane.   " I'd better go and see the police, or
they'll think I'm putting something across them."   He gave
a fleeting smile, and for once looked more like Richard than
like Martin.

He had hardly opened the study door when he heard
Richard say :

"Hallo, Maestro! We've just had a telephone call, Oakes is on the way from the Yard. Case of let 'em all come." He was smiling cheerfully, as if he knew that this would annoy the local police, and rejoiced. " Better wait for the great man before we confer, hadn't we ? "

17   NIGHT WATCH

FANE rubbed the back of his head as he went into the study, nodded at the Inspector, and sat at his own desk. The typewriter was pushed to one side, and there was a pile of pages, already typed, placed neatly in front of him ; a pen stood in a stand just by his side. Martin, studying him, wondered whether his father actually wished that he could get on with checking the work that he had written earlier in the day. He marvelled at his father's phenomenal powers of concentration ; Fane would say that he owed everything to that, and nothing to his style. If one believed him, he had a disparaging view of his work.

He fiddled with the pen.

Detective Inspector Cornley, of the Dorset C.I.D., knew Fane personally and by reputation. He was never at ease with a man whom he thought famous—or at least well known—without justification. Crime, to Cornley, was a serious business, and it shocked him that so many people read about it for amusement. He was a chunky man, with a square chin which came to an odd little point in the middle. Red-complexioned and with sandy hair, he looked an un-imaginative block, until one studied his small blue eyes : shrewd and penetrating eyes.

"Well, Inspector." Fane was always formal with this man. " I'm afraid it's a bad business. The driver is dead, of course. Killed so that he couldn't identify the gunman, possibly. Or instead of Miss Kennedy. I suppose that's any one's guess."

Fane was really saying that he wasn't interested in Cornley, and agreed with Richard that the best thing was to wait for the Yard man. His prosiness told the younger Fanes that he was impatient with the need for studying Cornley's feelings.   Richard gave Martin a surreptitious wink.

" Yes, he's dead," said Cornley.   " Which of you saw the murderer ? "

" I did," said Martin.

" Describe him, please."

" Small, thin, dressed in a raincoat, wearing a light-grey trilby hat," said Martin promptly.   " He was a hundred and fifty yards away, but I can tell you that he was thin, and I think his hair was black."

" How could you tell, if he wore a hat ? "

" He knocked it against the branch of a tree, and pushed it off his forehead."

Cornley was making notes ; but Cornley hadn't a man up here with him, which meant that the notes weren't really official.   Fane began to doodle, apparently taking little interest in the description.

" This Miss Kennedy," said Cornley.   " Do you know her ? "

" I've met her."

" Recently ? "

" You know," said Fane, in a voice which betrayed his impatience even more clearly, " I really think it would be much better if we wait until Mr. Oakes arrives.   It will save going over the same ground twice, won't it ? "   He lit another cigarette.   " He shouldn't be long."

Cornley didn't speak, just looked affronted.   What could have been an uncomfortable silence was broken by the telephone.   Fane stretched out for it, without looking at the policeman, whose little eyes were fixed on the instrument.

" Jonathan Fane here . . . Martin ? . . . Yes, he's here. Who is that, please ? . . . I see."   Fane handed the instrument across and said, " Fraser."

" Thanks."   Martin stood up, then leaned against the desk.   He wished Cornley weren't here ; he was never so much at ease with the police as his father or Richard. " Hallo, Fraser . . ."

Fraser said, " Is she all right ? "

" Perfectly all right."

" Not suffering any after-effects from that blow I gave her ? "

" None at all."

" Everything else all right ? "

Martin said, " No, I wouldn't say that, but you needn't worry about Rhoda. I'll be up first thing in the morning, and I'll see you then. I'll be here all night, if you need anything urgently."

There was silence at the other end of the wire, but he was sure that Fraser hadn't hung up. He waited impatiently; Cornley was staring with suspicious curiosity.

" What's the trouble ? " Fraser asked at last. " If that bitch of a woman has followed her—— "

" What makes you think she might have done ? "

" I can imagine she'd try," said Fraser. " Listen to me, Fane. I keep my head, most of the time, but every time I think of the Kennedy woman I lose it. She's dangerous, she's corrupt, and she means to do Rhoda harm."

" Could be," said Martin. He pictured the other man's face, could even imagine his tense expression. A handsome man, in a fashion; young; and in some ways too naïve to be true. His manner continually contradicted itself. " Listen, Fraser. If you really feel that, do something for me."

" What ? "

" Sit down and write out a report on her. Tell me exactly why you feel like that about her. And you might add this, too." Martin hesitated, anxious not to give anything away to Cornley, choosing his words. " In the bottom right-hand drawer of your desk you'll find an envelope with some Press cuttings. Have a look at them, and include all you can about them, will you ? "

Fraser said, " *What ?* " in a voice which rose upwards ludicrously.

" You don't think I spent my time there for nothing, do you ? " Martin said. " Will you have it ready for me to-morrow ? "

There was a pause; and then the last thing he expected: Fraser laughed—so loudly that he really seemed amused. It was several seconds before he was able to speak calmly.

" You beat the band," he said. " Right, I'll do that. If you're sure about Rhoda."

" I'm sure."

" I'll haunt you for the rest of your days if anything

happens to her." Fraser paused again, then added abruptly,
" Good night."

Martin hung up.

He had noticed the others moving, but hadn't paid them
much attention. Now he saw that Fane and Cornley had
left the room, and Richard was sitting in the easy-chair,
grinning all over his face. Martin went across and dropped
on to an upright chair.

" Mr. Discretion," said Richard. " Cornley was sprout-
ing ears to catch any word he could, but I don't think he
could have the faintest idea what you were talking about.
He probably thinks that Fraser works for us."

" He'll soon find out that he doesn't. What's happened ?"

" Oakes," said Richard simply.

" Already ! "

" Take it from me that Oakes will be in a good mood," said
Richard. " He always is, when Dad's about. Wouldn't
surprise me if he isn't a secret reader of thrillers. Hark at
'em ! " Men were talking in loud voices downstairs, and
there was a little outburst of laughter. " Thick as thieves.
I'll bet Cornley hates the sight of them both."

" He'll get over it," said Martin.

.   .   .   .   .

Chief Inspector Oakes of Scotland Yard was a big, barrel-
shaped man with a shock of iron-grey hair which stood
straight up from his forehead. His grey eyes, larger than
Cornley's, had much the same piercing brightness. He
came into the study behind Cornley and in front of Fane ;
and for the next hour he was amiable and inquiring, deferred
frequently to Cornley, and as often to Fane himself. He was
being himself—breathing innocence, a bluff and honest man
who wouldn't deceive a child. He had a hearty voice and a
hearty laugh, and was so used to murder that each new one
had little or no outward effect on him. Those who knew
him well knew that he was actually less cold-blooded than he
seemed ; and knew also that he could be a good friend.

He listened well.

The only time that he seemed startled was when Martin
told him that Rhoda Grenfell was here ; and why.

He laughed. " I suppose you're going to say that you

would have told me, whether this had happened or not."

"Might have," said Martin simply. "My father wanted me to."

"If you'd take your father's advice more often you wouldn't get yourself into so much trouble," said Oakes amiably. "I shouldn't have to get you out of it, either! Anyhow, we don't want the pretty Rhoda just yet." He laughed again—and laughed frequently during the hour.

He left, with Cornley and the other police, after a police-surgeon had seen Hilda Kennedy and agreed with Dr. Tucker, who had been and gone, that she was suffering from such severe shock that it was impossible to get any coherent story out of her. They did not even know why she had come to Nairn Lodge.

Fane saw them off, while Martin and Richard stayed in the study. Fane went into the morning-room before coming back, and the women's voices sounded. They grew louder.

Fane came back to the study.

"Miss Grenfell's going to bed in your room, Richard," he said. "You will have to shake down in one of the rooms on the third floor."

"Pleasure," said Richard, jumping up.

Rhoda said, "Good night. And—thank you."

She appeared in the doorway only for a moment. She seemed rested; much more reposeful than she had been all the day. Evelyn Fane went off with her, and Fane smiled faintly.

"Things going all right there," said Richard.

Fane closed the door.

"Yes, you young rip. Chiefly because your mother knows that you could easily be a suspect. I ought to warn you that when this affair is over there'll be a strong campaign to make you find some respectable way of earning a living. We needn't go into that now. What did Fraser want, Martin?"

Martin told him.

"Sounds reasonable," decided Fane. "I like that laughing business. Might be a nice young man. Well, Oakes couldn't have been more amenable, could he? I don't think there's much doubt that he had been in touch

with Dorchester earlier, and Cornley knew he was coming
down, or he couldn't have got here so soon. Cornley hoped
that the trouble here would enable him to steal a march."

" What a hope," said Richard. " With Oakes! "

" Yes," said Fane. His expression was hard to understand ; he seemed to ponder for a while, and then he turned
to Richard and spoke heavily, " Listen, Skip." It was a
childhood nickname, now seldom used. " It would be easy
to forget the most important thing about this to you—and to
all of us. The Grenfells, Fraser, Hilda Kennedy, and
everyone else who might be concerned don't rank anything
like so high. You saw a murder ; and you might be in
heavy weather, because it means you had the opportunity to
kill Rhoda's mother. You haven't forgotten that, have you ? "

Richard looked almost humble.

" Er—no. Going there was a crazy thing to do, but it
might have—— "

" Possibly it has worked a trick," said Fane. " I'm not
blaming you for it—I just wanted to make sure that both
of you realise that it has first priority. You may want to
solve the problem for the sake of what money you can get out
of it, but that's incidental. I don't want to see you in dock
on a charge of murder. And that leads to this." He
glanced at Martin. " You must be extremely careful how
you deal with the police. Be more than usually frank with
them. If they want anything, give it to them, unless it will
really get Richard in deeper. Understand ? "

Both nodded.

Fane leaned back, lit a cigarette, and smiled broadly.

" Sorry I had to read that section of the Riot Act. Parent's
privilege! Here's another. Richard, you look tired, and
that means you are tired, and you're to go to bed and sleep.
Scoop and I will be on duty."

Richard sat up. " What duty ? "

Fane shrugged.

" Watching Rhoda or Hilda ? " asked Martin.

Richard said, " My, my ! "

" I've had a few words with Tucker," said Fane. " He
says that Hilda Kennedy is putting up a wonderful act, but he
doesn't think that she's suffering from shock to anything like
the degree that she's making out. It's always hard to

diagnose. We've all pretended that we think she is, and the police have given her the benefit of the doubt. I think it's probable that she'll go into Rhoda's room during the night. That's why we've put Rhoda in Richard's room. There's the little dressing-room next to it, with the communicating door. Which watch will you take, Scoop? Now until three o'clock, or the second?"

"Second watch," said Martin promptly. "Starting at two, I shan't want more than a few hours' sleep. We young people can take it."

Fane chuckled. Richard protested—and went obediently to bed.

Ten minutes later the telephone bell rang, and Fane answered it. His eyes lit up.

"Hallo, Barbara, how are you? . . . Good! It's no use thinking Scoop's going to talk to you yet until you've told me what you've discovered about a star-gazer named Lena." He paused, beamed, and winked at Martin. "Yes, I told him you'd pick that up. Eh? . . . Oh, a Mrs. Lena *Farraday*."

Martin exclaimed, "What?"

"Quiet! Anything else . . . I see . . . committed suicide . . . oh . . . How long ago? . . . I see. All right, here's Scoop, he can't wait to say good night."

When Martin put down the receiver, two or three minutes later, his father said promptly:

"If you ever do anything without talking it over with Barbara, you'll be a fool. Now! If you're right and Fraser is also the Farraday of those Press cuttings, he's probably a relative of the Lena Farraday who made a big name for herself in South Africa as an astrologer, twenty years ago, kept it for ten years, and then committed suicide after she'd been proved a cheat and a fraud. That might explain a lot. I wonder if she ever knew Hilda Kennedy."

"I'll find out," said Martin heavily.

.   .   .   .   .

Training had taught Martin the trick of waking at whatever time he liked. He undressed and was in bed by half-past eleven, thinking of the Lena Farraday story; and he was sitting up, bleary-eyed, at five minutes to two. His mother had put a vacuum flask of tea by the bedside, with two cups. He poured one, put the stopper back in the flask, and dressed. His father was sitting in the little drawing-room at a card table, with a reading-lamp on it, poring over typewritten pages, content to work.   Martin stood watching him and grinning.

Fane yawned, winked, and stood up ; they didn't utter a word.   None was needed ; there had been no effort to visit Rhoda, if there had been Fane would have had plenty to say.   He squeezed Martin's shoulder, in lieu of saying good night, and went out.   Martin sat down at the card-table. He turned over the story Barbara had unearthed, and rejected any doubts that Fraser, alias Farraday, was a relative ; perhaps a son.   Soon his gaze fell on his father's manuscript, and he began to read.   It was the middle of a Prince story, that day's work, and there were surprisingly few alterations in the typing.   Here and there Fane had corrected a page extensively in a small, sometimes untidy, but always legible hand.

The room was warm, with an electric fire.   Martin lit his pipe, and went on reading.   His father had an easy style, which was why he was so widely read ; and incident piled upon incident.   Now and again, Martin found himself grinning.   As often, he told himself that his job was to watch and listen, he mustn't let himself be carried away. He still kept reading.   The only striking clock in the house, a centuries-old grandfather, boomed three ; he was surprised that the hour had passed so quickly.

His pipe was out.   He scraped it cautiously, and stood up to stretch his legs.

He heard a creak—of door or floorboard, he couldn't be sure which.

18   NIGHT TALK

MARTIN switched off the fire and the reading-lamp which his father had shaded so that no light would show at the doors ; the passage door wasn't latched.   Martin reached it as he heard another creak ; the floorboards in the passage weren't too good. He opened the door an inch or two, and peered out. Light from the landing cast a dim glow. He saw a shadowy figure approaching, one hand outstretched.

Sleep-walking?

He didn't give that possibility much thought. Hilda Kennedy was wearing one of his mother's dressing-gowns and a pair of her slippers, and staring at the door of the room opposite: a box-room. She turned to it and opened it, cautiously, then peered inside. She would find only trunks and cases and oddments. Martin crossed to the door which communicated with Rhoda's room, opened it an inch, and stood by, leaning slightly against the wall. That would be more comfortable if this proved a long vigil.

He heard the creaking again; Rhoda's was the next room that the older woman would try.

Martin's heart was thumping in an odd, uneven way; it wasn't excitement so much as nervousness. He had been pushed around so much in this case; nothing had gone according to plan. Now, it was possible that Hilda Kennedy meant to kill. Undoubtedly Fraser thought so.

The door of the next room opened, with a slight squeak. A thin beam from a torch showed. He saw it wandering about the room, always at the same level; then it stopped.

Hilda had seen Rhoda.

He heard a rustling, then a click, of the door being closed. The light didn't go out. After what seemed a long moment, a brighter light went on—the ceiling-lamp, which was very bright; Richard hated a poor light. Now Martin could see the head of Rhoda's bed. Nice work on his father's part; the bed could be seen easily from this door.

Hilda appeared, one hand still outstretched. She was full face for a moment, and gradually turned until she was three-quarter face towards Martin. She didn't glance his way; if she did, all she would see was a door, ajar. She appeared to be oblivious of everything but Rhoda. She approached to within a few feet of the bed, and stopped. Her hands were at her breast, the tips of the fingers touching, strangely like an attitude of prayer. She didn't look plain now; he remembered how distinguished he had thought her when she had been sitting in front of the crystal star.

She went nearer.

Had she a weapon ? Was this an errand of murder ? If it were, would she waste so much time ?

She stretched out her right hand and touched the bed, near Rhoda's waist.

Rhoda stirred. The other woman didn't move, but her eyes were wide open and her gaze fixed all the time on Rhoda's face. Rhoda stirred again, turned on her back, turned to her side again. She became restless. Her left arm appeared from beneath the bedclothes ; Martin thought that her eyelids fluttered.

Throughout all this there was no change in Hilda's attitude ; she stood with uncanny stillness.

Rhoda opened her eyes.

She closed them quickly, against the bright light, but she was awake, and re-opened them slowly, putting up one hand to keep the light off. Hilda moved, so that she cast a shadow on the girl. Martin could only see her profile now ; he wanted to see more. He moved his position slightly, but it didn't help.

" Hilda," said Rhoda with a sighing tone. " Hilda." The name just reached Martin's ears.

" I've come, you see," said Hilda.

" I'm—glad." Rhoda's voice was low.

" Do you want me to stay here ? "

" Yes, please." Rhoda's voice became stronger. " But go now—we'll talk to-morrow."

" Yes," said Hilda. She paused. " Someone tried to kill me."

" I know," said Rhoda. " I'm—sorry." Then, " Please go, Hilda—there's no danger now. We'll talk again to-morrow."

For a moment Hilda stood there in silence ; then, with a swift movement, she turned to the door. The light went out, and the door closed gently. The floorboards creaked. Martin crept across to the passage door and opened it in time to see Hilda Kennedy going into her own room. That light went out, and silence settled on the house.

Martin went back to the little room, closed the door into Rhoda's room, switched on the reading-lamp and fire, and sat down, but he was no longer interested in the manuscript. He stared at it without reading. The talk in the night had that quality of unreality which he now associated with Hilda Kennedy. He had heard every word and seen both women, yet it seemed like something he had heard and seen in a dream. That was partly because it had been so unexpected. He couldn't imagine anything less sinister. And Hilda, far from dominating Rhoda, had seemed almost—submissive. That was probably the effect of her narrow escape, Martin decided.

Danger and the likelihood of anything else happening to-night seemed gone. It was a quarter to four. He would have to stay, but he started to yawn. Tension had kept him wide awake, but he wasn't anything like as alert as he had been.

He lit his pipe, poured out another cup of tea, and tried to read the story again; it didn't hold him. He stood up, and walked round the room several times, breathing in deeply; he must keep himself awake. The fire wasn't helping. He turned it off, and within a few minutes coldness crept into the room, it wouldn't be long before he began to shiver.

He switched the fire on again, and turned and looked towards the passage door.

It was opening slowly.

Martin moved swiftly to the wall behind the door, hand in his pocket, about his gun. The door opened a foot or so, then stopped. After a few seconds a man whispered:

" Scoop. You there ? "

It was Richard.

Martin moved away from the door and took his hand out of his pocket. Richard heard the movement, poked his head into the room, grinned, and stepped inside. His hair was tousled, he wore the same clothes as during the day, with a thick polo sweater on top. His eyes were bright and no longer bloodshot.

" Scare you ? "

" Yes."

" Sorry. My turn of duty. Any alarums and excursions ? "

" Nothing much."

" Meaning something ? " Richard's voice rose.

" Pipe down," said Martin. " Wait a minute." He went to Rhoda's door and listened; there was no sound, she had probably dropped off to sleep again.   He waited for several seconds, then went back to his chair.

Richard joined him, sitting on the edge of the bed.   He was looking down at the manuscript.

"Was he *work*ing?" Richard asked, pointing to the manuscript.

Martin nodded.

"Someone called that man an industrious fantast, which wasn't far wrong," said Richard, almost in horror.   "Bless his old cotton socks, he's never once told me that the only way to succeed is by hard work."

"He's probably given up hope!"

Richard grimaced, and lit a cigarette.   Martin told him what had happened, and found him mildly incredulous. Martin, wide awake now, watched his brother closely. Richard was in a good and probably an expansive mood. He was satisfied with himself, because he had come to take over the watch.   In a few minutes he would shoo Martin out of the room, and laugh at any suggestion that he ought to go back to bed.

Martin had plenty on his mind about Richard.

"Skip," he said, about to tell of Lena Farraday's history.

Richard's eyes rounded.   "Hal-*lo*!   Homily in the offing, with a beginning like that."   He smiled.   "I'm strong and healthy, I can take it, but no—I won't promise to be good."

Martin grinned, in spite of himself.

"Before you go on," said Richard, "one or two little notions I've been having.   About Grenfell.   I don't get Grenfell's position in this.   Seems phoney.   He could pay one of his star crime reporters a handsome bonus, and make sure that the investigation was done by experts.   Why come to us?   If he did come, that is; if he didn't just follow Rhoda.   I think we ought to dig as deep as we can and find out if his finances are sound.   If they're not—he'll probably benefit from the death of Rhoda and her mother.   Anyhow, he might.   Worth digging?"

"Of course.   I doubt if we'd find the evidence, even if it exists, but we might try."

"Friend of mine works for him," said Richard airily. "I was going to get some results all on my own, but after the second murder I think you'd better come into the picture.

As a matter of fact, I was damned peeved the night before last night, when I might have come across. You put me off by your censorious attitude!"

Martin broke in abruptly. Richard might have something worth saying, but was more likely talking for the sake of talking; he had probably assumed that the subject of the girl in Fulham would crop up; so it could come up, this was as good a time as any. If Richard had been seen at The Grove and the Yard started to question the family, danger might become acute.

"Leave it for a minute. There's something else to talk about. That girl in Fulham—what's her name?"

Richard's grin was almost as wide as Sampson's.

"I *thought* so. You mean June Grey. *Very* nice girl, June Grey. Not a rival for Kathleen though; believe it or not, I'm fidelity itself. June works for Grenfell, she's the second of his three secretaries. Now faint."

19   TRIUMPH FOR RICHARD

THEY were talking in whispers; that didn't make the shock any less. Martin looked incredulous. " I don't believe it " was on the tip of his tongue, but he kept it back. Richard beamed, looking boyish in his triumph. He lit another cigarette and stood up. He backed towards Rhoda's door, watching Martin all the time, put a finger to his lips, and listened. He returned slowly.

" She's still asleep, the pretty. Well."

" I don't get it," said Martin woodenly.

" That's because you don't appreciate my value to Prince," said Richard with mock earnestness. " Or my willingness to work like a cart-horse in order to make the show pay—and get myself out of the red, incidentally. Had a chance meeting with June a few weeks ago, as I told you. Chatted over a cup of tea, as a matter of fact, and she told me who she worked for. Er—I knew beforehand, I'd done some research work."

Martin just sat and listened.

" Don't get me wrong," said Richard. " I'm no star-gazer, and I didn't study my horoscope. I'd just had an idea. You know that the *Sunday Clarion* runs a Missing Persons feature. Trace your long-lost relatives through the all-embracing columns of the *Clarion*, so to speak."

" I did vaguely."

" You should have known more," said Richard reprovingly. " Private detectives ought to know everything. Anyway, the *Clarion* does. I had this notion. If we could get tied up with the *Clarion*, do some of its investigations—I believe it uses some of its own staff and some outside people —we might pay ourselves very nicely, thank you. I sounded the Maestro, and learned that he knew Grenfell slightly. Sold him some murky mysteries, of course! I thought that might come in handy later, but I wanted to fix this for myself. Alone I did it." He struck a Napoleonic attitude. " See the point? Sleeping partner wakes every one up. Dull-witted Richard ends worries of Prince Agency. Addle-pate makes good. I might inform you," he added, and there was a serious note in his voice and look in his eyes, " that I have not felt like rejoicing at my recent share in the work, or the fact that I'm always owing Prince money. I took myself to task. This seemed the needed brain-wave. So I cultivated June. Honestly, though. No hint of romance or that kind of thing. In fact, I gave her one of Dad's books and a copy of one of Kath's photographs, both autographed—she's a film fan in a nice way as well as a thriller fan. Told her who I was and what I wanted, too. All on the up-and-up, you see."

Martin said heavily, " You young devil! "

" That's right." Richard grinned delightedly. " How was I to know that it might come in useful, one day? Long arm of coincidence, eh? I went to Fulham this—no, yesterday—morning, to have a word with June. I wanted a refuge—and I thought I might learn something from June about Grenfell's movements. No results there, though. I've met her people, nice folk, by the way, although she's streets ahead of the others, in some ways. They gave her a special education, and—as you were! We want to know more about Grenfell's financial position. June is one of his secretaries. So if you don't mind my going back to London——"

" You go where you like," said Martin faintly.

" Oh, only after the closest consultation with the Boss! Mind you, nothing guaranteed. June might not buy this one. She's very straight, has clear ideas of right and wrong and all that kind of thing. I think you'd get a shock if you met June."

" I don't want any more shocks."

Richard said slowly, " It might work, mightn't it? It's worth trying, anyhow."

" It couldn't be better."

" Thanks," said Richard. " Have to make sure now that Grenfell doesn't discover that I'm friendly with June. Incidentally, he's a good employer and calls her Miss Grey. No sit-on-my-knee-pat-pat-squeeze-squeeze from Grenfell. Thing is, what to tell June? "

" Think you can trust her? "

" I've been trying to tell you so," said Richard plaintively.

" Then tell her it's part of the inquiry into his sister-in-law's death. How does she feel about Prince? "

Richard forgot to keep his voice low, and chuckled.

" She's such a Prince fan—the Maestro's version, I mean —that she's half-way there already, I'd say. Promised her that one day she would shake hands with the author. I don't think it would have been so easy without that." He considered. " You may be right, too—tell her everything, cards on the table. Yes. Care to see her yourself? "

" Care to let me? "

" Don't be humble," said Richard. " The pose may convince strangers, but it misses with me. You have as much conceit as the Maestro, the only thing that makes you both different from other men is that you hide it so nicely. Yes, I think it would be a good idea if you were to see her. Better if the Maestro would."

" He will."

" You fix it," said Richard. " And make sure that you put me in a good light with him. Budding genius, and all that kind of thing. After all, we might flop on this case, and I shall have to go to him for a pony to help me over." He stood up, smiling. " Lord, it's nearly five! How long do you mean to stay up? *I'm* on duty."

" Here's something to keep you awake," said Martin, and at last told the story of Lena Farraday and Fraser's possible *alias*.

Richard looked more thoughtful, as if this angle of the case had taken the edge off his appetite for Grenfell.

. . . . .

Martin went back to bed, thoughtful at first, then gay with the false vitality of early morning. He chuckled to himself a dozen times before he dropped off to sleep.

It was nearly eight when he woke up, to find his mother by the side of his bed, holding a big cup of steaming tea. She was in a dressing-gown, but had made up a little. He struggled up and took the tea. She leaned forward and kissed his forehead.

" All quiet ? " he asked.

" Yes. I couldn't sleep well, and I went along to Richard at six o'clock," said Evelyn Fane. " I couldn't make him go to bed, but he might as well have gone. Every one's all right. Rhoda has just woken, Miss Kennedy's awake and seems much better."

" Any news of Sampson ? "

" Yes, I telephoned as soon as I woke up. He's had a fair night, and he's not on the danger-list."

" Thank God for that," Martin said quietly.

His mother said, " Yes." Then paused and added in a brisker voice, " Your father looks as if he hasn't had any sleep for a week. Was he *working* last night ? "

The insistence in her eyes reminded him of the way she had looked when demanding the truth from him as a child.

" Yes," said Martin.

Evelyn caught her breath. " He's impossible ! Bless him." She sat on the side of the bed and watched her son steadily, and he knew that she hadn't yet spoken of the heaviest load on her mind. " Scoop."

" Hm-hm ? "

" Do you really *like* this work ? "

Martin said slowly, " Well, yes, I suppose I do. It has a something which gets into you. I'm not good at it, but I'm learning. I'd rather do it than anything else, even though there are bad times. Like yesterday."

" I see," she said slowly. " And Richard ? "

" He couldn't be keener."

" Is he *really* in danger ? "

" He could be," said Martin, " but I don't think it will get really bad. Richard's sounder than some of us think."

" You needn't tell me that," said Evelyn, her voice more brisk. " Richard's all right." She took the empty cup and stood up. " All right, Scoop. Only be careful, won't you ? "

Martin stopped her, with a hand on her arm.

" Just a minute," he said, and smiled, but there was no amusement in his eyes. They watched each other steadily, and when he spoke he chose his words carefully, " What do you really think about it ? "

" Would that make any difference ? "

" It might."

Evelyn said, " I hate it, most of the time. Then I remember that sometimes you do a lot of good, and I tell myself that obviously you're cut out for it, so I'll have to stand by and let it go on. Only be *very* careful."

" All the time," Martin promised.

. . . . .

Oakes of the Yard was still in the district, and arrived with Cornley just after half-past nine. He had no objection to the Fane brothers going back to London. He questioned Hilda Kennedy, who seemed more genuinely tired this morning than she had been the night before. Oakes and Cornley obviously thought that she was in danger. Men were to be left in the grounds, and one would be in the house, taking Sampson's place temporarily.

Rhoda was obviously content to stay, but seemed in no hurry to talk to Hilda.

All the men of the Fane family left by road, just after half-past ten, Fane driving his own car with Richard beside him, Martin driving the Buick.

. . . . .

Jonathan Fane and Martin went to Quill House, while Richard went to get in touch with June Grey. Jessica was working at the records when the two entered, and jumped up, flushing with embarrassment at sight of Jonathan, who always tried to put her at her ease, but never wholly succeeded. Barbara, in the doorway of her office and looking bright-eyed and well, chuckled as they entered. Martin kissed her.

" What's funny ? "

" The only people who can make Jessica blush are your father and policemen," she said.

" We've a lot in common," said Fane, and kissed her cheek. " I needn't ask you if you've really recovered, after the way you showed Scoop up. Nasty thing, this 'flu." He sat down; he seldom stood for a moment if he could avoid it. " What else have you got to tell us ? "

" I suppose you know the whole story ? "

Fane nodded.

" Well, only one new thing has happened," said Barbara, still lightly. " I don't know how Scoop does it, but he's managed to get Reginald Fraser eating out of his hand. He's coming here at half-past two. He says he has that report ready, and that it's past time you gave him some real work to do. I like him," she added decidedly.

" You keep away from him," said Martin.

" I wonder if he'll confess to being Farraday," Fane mused. "All right, all right, don't tell me that I'm only guessing he is !"

" What's been happening with you ? " Barbara asked.

They had told her of the murder, by telephone; all that was left was the incident during the night, Oakes's friendly attitude that morning; and about Richard's scheming with June. Barbara looked as incredulous as Martin had been.

" Biggest danger you have is under-estimating Richard," said Fane. " I'll be a lot happier when this is cleared up, though, and we don't have to worry about the police wanting to know why he was at Mrs. Grenfell's flat. However ! It's a quarter to two, and we haven't had lunch yet. Have you ?"

" Yes."

" I'll have a sandwich in the office," said Martin. " I don't want to miss Fraser at two-thirty. You go and have lunch and be back by half-past."

" Right ! " Fane, a good trencherman, went out. Martin and Barbara looked through the morning's post, which wasn't exciting. They discussed everything that had happened, without getting any farther. They were still discussing it at twenty minutes past two, when Richard's voice sounded in the outer office, followed by a girl's.

June Grey was here.

.   .   .   .   .

Her voice gave Martin his first surprise. He had expected her to speak with a quasi-cultured voice, with an undertone of Cockney. Instead, she had a naturally pleasant speaking voice. He was excited at the thought of meeting her—perhaps more than the circumstances warranted. Richard pushed the door of his office wide open, and called:

" June Grey, folk ! "

She was tall, and dressed in a tweed two-piece suit with gauntlet gloves and heavy walking-shoes; just right for the cold day. She wore a close-fitting hat, which suited her. She might have stepped out of the pages of *Vogue*, or off the screen. Even the thick tweed couldn't disguise her figure; in spite of her height, she was superbly built. Her hair was auburn, her eyes green-grey. She reminded Martin of his mother, except that she was really beautiful, in an almost classical way. Her movements were easy, and obviously she felt no embarrassment.

Richard chuckled.

" Everyone duly shaken ? "

" Don't be absurd, Richard," said June Grey lightly.

" You see," said Richard, " she puts me in my place even better than you two do. Well, here we are. We've had a chat, and in principle it's agreed—June will try to find out if there's anything rocky with the *Clarion* or with Grenfell's private affairs. Aren't I good ? "

June said, " You're too good. You know—— "

" But you haven't really been introduced," said Richard. " My brother Martin and Barbara Mallison, his fiancée. Now every one knows every one else ! What were you going to say ? "

" That I can't promise anything," said June promptly. " I don't know what Richard's told you, but I don't know any way of waving a wand and finding out all this, you know. I think it's worth doing, I—well, I'd rather like to try. But it mightn't succeed."

" Of course not," said Barbara. " We try ten things for every one that comes off. We all know that."

" Except Richard," said June, and set the others laughing. " There's another thing, too. I'm not sure that I know how to set about it. Richard talks a lot of nonsense, but I'm hoping that you'll be able to give me some intelligent advice."

" I dislike auburn hair," announced Richard.

" How long can you spare now ? " asked Martin.

" I'm free until four o'clock."

" Good—that's plenty of time."

Martin glanced up as he heard the outer office door open ; and a moment later, heard his father's voice, followed by Reggie Fraser's ; they had come up the stairs together. Fane would bring Fraser right in ; he hadn't wanted June and Fraser to meet so soon. Fraser might not be all he seemed. He jumped up quickly and went towards the door, and the telephone bell rang as he reached it. Then the door opened, and Fraser was ahead of Fane ; he couldn't miss seeing June, and the damage was done. Probably it would come to nothing.

Jessica called, " It's for Mr. Jonathan—Mrs. Fane."

" Oh. Thanks," said Fane. He was looking intently at June. " Introduce every one, Scoop." He picked up the telephone and sank into a chair. " Hallo, my sweet."

He sat up slowly ; his expression altered, and none of the others liked what they saw. Martin and Richard made no attempt to introduce June and Fraser.

Fane said slowly, " Well, there it is. I'm sorry, darling. I'll be back as soon as I can. Yes—I won't lose a minute."

He replaced the receiver, took out cigarettes, looked straight into Martin's eyes, and said :

" Hilda Kennedy died half an hour ago. Poisoning is suspected."

20   FRASER'S REPORT

No one spoke ; for a while there seemed to be nothing to say. Fraser looked as surprised as any of them, only June looked shocked. It was June, glancing from one man to the other and then to Barbara, who broke the silence.

" Does he mean *the* Hilda Kennedy ? "

" Oh, yes," Richard piped up. " The teller of fortunes to the masses. Did you know her ? "

" Yes," said June. " It's awful."

Fane put both hands to his forehead and brushed the hair back. He looked grave, and older. Every one waited for him to speak, and he seemed to realise that they were hanging on his words. He was a long time speaking—and before any word came a smile began to play about the corners of his lips.

" Don't make any mistake," he said. " I'm no oracle, and I can't explain this. I must get back to your mother, boys." He only occasionally used the term " boys "; then only absently. " How well did you know her, June ? "

" Not really well," June said. " I knew a great deal about her. This will upset Sir Edward dreadfully."

" Is Grenfell fond of her ? " Fane's voice sharpened ; he would be remembering that Grenfell had made a great show of his suspicions of Hilda.

" Well, I suppose so, in a way," June said. " I wasn't meaning personally. He's always believed that she is one of the paper's most important contributors—she has millions of followers. She'd become almost a tradition, of course."

" I see." Fane ran his hands over his head again. " I must get away, but before I go—June, look at me."

The girl was looking at him, and her lovely eyes did not waver. When he liked, Fane could be compelling ; only Richard would have dared to interrupt then, and even he was subdued and silent.

" Two women have died in this business," said Fane in a matter-of-fact voice. " Others have been in danger. I think you ought to consider your position closely, June. It isn't just a game. You may find yourself in grave danger. I don't want either Richard or Martin to take the responsibility if that should come. You must decide for yourself. If I were you, I should back out. No one would think any the worse of you."

June didn't speak.

" He's right," Barbara said decidedly.

" Only thing to do," said Martin. " I'll be sorry, but——" He broke off, and shrugged.

Fraser was looking at the girl. He hadn't spoken a word since he had come in. His gaze had a curious intensity ; Martin found himself wondering why. Were they old acquaintances ? Nothing suggested it. Did Fraser know the girl by sight? Or know who she was? Or was he simply anxious to find out what was going on?

June said, " Mr. Fane, do you think that I might help to solve the mystery? Find out who killed Mrs. Grenfell and Hilda Kennedy."

" There's a chance, no more. But—— "

" I'd like to take the chance," said June.

" Attagirl! " breathed Richard.

" I'd give it more thought, if I were you," advised Fane. " Don't pay too much attention to Richard—unless it's to do the opposite of anything he advises! " He smiled at Richard and went to the door, his sons with him. Barbara, June, and Fraser were left in the office. Fraser had relaxed, and was smiling.

June said, " I can come back later, if it will help."

" Better stay," said Barbara; and laughed. " Of course, you two don't know each other. Mr. Reginald Fraser, Miss June Grey."

Martin was coming back and in the doorway when the couple looked at each other, murmuring polite acknowledgment. He felt sure that June was looking at a complete stranger; he wasn't so sure about Fraser, whose lips were curved.

" Barbara," Martin said, " you know pretty well what we'd like Miss Grey to do. Will you brief her? "

" Of course. My room's across here." Barbara took the younger girl out quickly.

Fraser had both hands in his pockets and looked at Martin quizzically. Martin didn't speak until Richard came back.

" You've guessed who this is."

" The junior partner," said Fraser.

" Knives? " asked Richard. " Guns? Or just bare fists? "

" When we've finished with the nonsense, let's get down to cases," said Martin. They sat down. " I gather you've been busy with the report, Fraser. Do you think it will take us any farther? Or has the latest development changed things? "

Fraser said frankly, " It's turned me head over heels. I suppose there isn't any chance that your father's wrong, is there? He wasn't pulling a fast one, to try to make me let my hair down."

"He was not." Martin fingered his pipe. "This is the second time something like this has happened at home when we've been on a job. He takes a lot of things lightly, but not murder. Hilda Kennedy's dead all right."

"Which makes her victim, not villainess," mused Fraser. "I'm inclined to give up."

"Why were you so down on her?"

Fraser pursed his lips.

"Partly because of her influence on Rhoda, of course. I've been quite sure that it was a bad one. True, I——"

"Did you know Rhoda before she met Hilda?"

"Well, no."

"Get someone to tell you what she was like," advised Martin heavily.

"Oh, I know the gossip." Fraser shrugged. "It comes to every one with a lot of money and some looks. Especially to someone who's had her own way as much as Rhoda. But it went deeper than that. I'd spend a few hours with Rhoda, and she'd be as happy and cheerful as any one could be. Gay as a cricket. Then she'd see Hilda, and——" He broke off, scowling. "I wish you'd seen the transformation. She would become silent, almost morose. Not herself. As if someone had taken possession of her. Call me crazy."

"Is that all?" asked Martin evenly.

"Taken over a period of months, and with it happening three or four times a week, it's plenty." Fraser stood up and began to walk about the office, touching papers and oddments, but watching Martin most of the time. "There were a hundred little indications that Hilda Kennedy's influence was bad. And there was the other gossip about Hilda. Gossip, I said. Scandal, I should have said."

"What is it?"

"Do you keep your eyes closed all the time?"

"I want to know what you think you know."

"Oh, well," said Fraser. "I've heard it from a dozen people that trusting maidens—not all of them young—who've let Hilda Kennedy tell their fortunes, have lost packets of money. Big packets. She's getting herself quite a reputation; at least, she was."

"Any proof?"

Fraser shook his head, and said, " But I still believe it."

" So do others," said Martin cryptically. " Anything else, Fraser ? "

" Not specific," said Fraser. He was speaking cautiously, and was not being wholly frank. Martin felt sure of that. " I knew her slightly. I didn't like her. I looked on her as a charlatan, of course, so I was prejudiced."

" Handsome of you to admit it," murmured Richard.

" It's all in here," Fraser took a foolscap envelope out of his pocket. " Chapter and verse, as far as I can give it to you. Several instances of what I mean by the change in Rhoda, after she'd seen her girl-friend. There's another note, too—that Hilda seemed pretty sure that Rhoda's mother was in danger, and I don't think she saw that in the stars. I suppose you'll tell me that she could have." He shrugged. " Satisfied ? "

" Not quite. Those Press cuttings of yours."

Fraser didn't answer at once. Richard lit a cigarette and went across and looked out of the window, without saying a word. Martin's face was set, and he looked remarkably like his father at the time that telephone call had come through.

Fraser said evenly, " What makes you think it will help, if I tell you ? "

" I think it might help to put you in the clear—or on the spot. You changed your name from Farraday, didn't you ? "

Fraser was hard-voiced.

" Yes. My business. Nothing criminal."

" No one said it was. There's nothing criminal in astrology, unless it's turned to criminal advantage. Lena Farraday was good, wasn't she ? As an astrologer, I mean."

Fraser sat down slowly. He looked as if he were trying to make up his mind to face an unpleasant task.

" I don't know. I once thought so." He paused, then went on harshly, " She was my mother. She really believed in her powers—once. My father died. Mother—married again. In South Africa." The words came out slowly, as if speaking hurt him. " She married the brother of Hilda Kennedy. The brother was a blackguard. He overcame my mother's scruples, and cheated a lot of people—on my mother's advice, taken from the stars, she said, they put money in fraudulent schemes. My stepfather cleaned up nicely, and then when the police started inquiring, he left her stranded." Fraser broke off with a harsh, "Need any more?"

"Everything, please," Martin said quietly.

Fraser lit another cigarette.

"My mother killed herself, after the police had virtually accused her. Her husband didn't live long—he died in an accident a few months later. He left his money to his sister, Hilda. I've always assumed that Hilda Kennedy was a fraud. I came to England years ago, changed my name, and tried to find evidence that would send her to gaol. I couldn't, but that didn't alter my conviction. Then— through tailing her, ironically—I met Rhoda. The thought that Rhoda was under that woman's influence—— "

He stopped abruptly.

Into the silence that followed Martin said:

"I can understand a lot now."

"Can you?" Fraser was taut.

"I think so. You hated Hilda Kennedy, who's been murdered."

Fraser actually smiled, although with an effort.

"I didn't hate Rhoda's mother. I didn't kill either of them. I just couldn't bear the thought that Rhoda was under her thumb, and—well, I tried to separate them. You know how brilliantly I succeeded." There was bitterness in his voice. "If you have any idea that I'm after Rhoda for her money, forget it. I'm more than comfortably off. My father was in gold, in Johannesburg's richest days."

"What did you do, in South Africa?"

"I sold out my father's business, did some big-game hunting, and fooled around." Fraser was abrupt. "All this can be proved."

"I'm sure it can," Martin said.

Fraser said quietly, "Thanks. Don't let us get too gloomy. Old wounds don't hurt all the time. You heard me tell Rhoda I couldn't go on, if she stuck to Hilda Kennedy. I meant it, but not because of Hilda. I simply couldn't go on with any one who was incurably obsessed by horoscopes. When I hit Rhoda, I broke something. In a way, I wish I'd let her go. Call me—callous. Call me what the hell you like, but—— " He broke off.

" Anything else ? " he asked abruptly, a moment later.

" Not now, thanks."

" Nothing I can do ? "

" Not yet."

Fraser said, " If I can help Rhoda, I will."   He went out, leaving the envelope containing his report on Martin's desk.

    ·   ·   ·   ·   ·

Richard was the first to break the silence after Fraser had gone.

" I must say I like the cut of his jib."

" People take to you at first sight, too," said Martin dryly.   He was frowning, and looking through the report. The quiet in the office was oppressive.   Richard began to move about, and suddenly said :

" I believed him."

" So did I."

" About the not-guilty plea, too ? "

Martin said, " I don't know.   I'd say he hated Hilda. If that were the only crime—— "

" More work to do," said Richard moodily.   " I seem to get farther and farther away from Grenfell.   What's your next move ? "

" A word with Kelby at the Yard, I think," Martin said. " Dad's advice of taking them into our confidence is as good as it can be.   It would be easy to leave it until it's too late."

He actually stretched out his hand for the telephone when the outer office door opened.   A moment later the deep, hard voice of Superintendent Kelby of Scotland Yard sounded, asking for Richard.

Richard said softly, " Why me ?   Why not the Boss ? "

21   BAD FOR RICHARD ?

" YES, sir," said Jessica, and the Fane brothers could imagine her blushing.   " I think he's in, I'll just find out. Won't you take a seat ? "

" Hurry, please," said Kelby.

Martin went to the door as the telephone bell rang. He didn't like this development; and Richard certainly wouldn't. The eye-witnessing of the murder sprang to the surface of their minds. Martin liked Kelby least of the three policemen he usually dealt with—Oakes and Wimple were the others. Kelby hadn't any patience with free-lance agents.

Kelby stood plump and massive; he had a fat chin, was ruddy of face and almost bald. He was dressed, as usual, in heavy brown tweeds, but wore no overcoat. Wimple, a big man, looked like a stripling beside him.

Martin reached the door.

" Hallo, Fane," Kelby said. " Your brother in ? "

Richard's voice came from the telephone.

" Yes. Come in," said Martin. He led the way into the office, and Richard put down the receiver and raised a hand in welcome, without a hint of anxiety.

" Hallo, hallo ! All the great men foregather on this job. Aren't we having a time, Superintendent ? "

" Yes, aren't we," said Kelby. He motioned to Wimple, who slid a note-book out of his pocket. " I want to ask you a few questions, Mr. Fane. You won't mind if I have the answers noted ? "

" Great Scott, no ! Everything for the record. What have I done wrong now ? "

" Where were you the night before last, Mr. Fane ? "

Martin felt his heart thump, but kept a poker face. Richard's beam faded into a frown, as if he were trying to recollect what had happened. Then he brightened.

" Oh, yes. The night before last. I paid a visit to Hilda Kennedy and—— "

" I know about that. Later."

Richard said, " I went back to our flat."

" Do you know what time ? "

" I'm poor at records," said Richard. " My brother probably knows exactly."

" Tennish," said Martin.

" And what did you do then ? "

" Went to bed, nursing injured vanity."

" And what time did you get up ? "

Richard said, " You're so full of questions." He lit a

cigarette and blew smoke towards the ceiling, watched by the others.

Martin could have steered the questions for the time being, but left this to Richard.   Richard took a long time answering, but Kelby didn't prompt him again ; Kelby expected a lie.

Richard said, " Oh, hell ! But you'd better know.   I was brilliant.   I went to see Mrs. Grenfell.   I was there when she was killed.   In the room.   Eye-witness."

Wimple exclaimed, " No ! "

Kelby was obviously dumbfounded, glared at Wimple, gave himself time to recover, and growled :

" Got that, Sergeant ? "

Wimple's pencil was speeding.   " Yes, sir."

" Did you know this ? "   Kelby turned to Martin.

Martin didn't answer.

" Now don't try to bring the family into it," protested Richard.   " It was my brain-wave, and Martin was annoyed because I didn't stay in bed like a good boy.   Yes, I saw it happen.   Take this down, Sergeant, will you ? "

He told the story again, quietly.   Kelby didn't ask a single question when he had finished, but looked puzzled, certainly not accusing.   Wimple was obviously distressed. Martin, blank-faced as he watched his brother, knew that Jonathan Fane would have liked to see Richard then.

" That's the lot," Richard said.   " How much did you know ? "   He was almost impish.

" We were told that you'd been seen near Mrs. Grenfell's flat," Kelby said.   " Never mind who told us.   Where did you go afterwards ? "

" Forget it," said Richard.

Kelby usually pressed every point home as far as it would go.   He missed, this time ; he hadn't been prepared for anything so clear as this.   Martin was thinking that the story sounded thin ; the telling rather than the details themselves made it convincing.   Two masked men, one big, one small . . .

Kelby said, " You'll come along with me, Mr. Fane, of course."

" Oh.   Yes.   Darbies ? "

" I hope you won't be foolish enough to run away," growled Kelby heavily.

"He won't." Martin was brisk. "Like a lawyer, Richard?"

"Oh, not at this stage," said Richard. "I don't think I'll need one, either. Up to the police to find the little chap who did the deed." His voice sharpened. "Charging me, Superintendent?"

"Not yet," said Kelby.

.   .   .   .   .

The office seemed empty.

Barbara and June were still in the other room, which was nearer soundproof than this; Barbara had no idea what had happened. Martin sat with his empty pipe between his teeth, looking at the wall. His father had been right, he was more often right than wrong. The urgent need was to find the killer, for Richard's sake; for the family's sake.

There was no need to tell his mother or father yet. They had plenty to worry about at Nairn Lodge. With luck, Richard's detention wouldn't get into the newspapers; certainly it wouldn't be in them until the morning, so there was a night to work in.

Would Kelby charge Richard?

He would probably prefer a simple charge, like breaking and entering, as an excuse to hold Richard. Kelby wouldn't mind if the case broke the Prince Agency. Kelby wouldn't close the agency down without a good case, but he'd be glad when it shut its doors.

The door opened after a timid tap.

"Yes, Jessica?" He looked up into the girl's pale face. "What is it?"

"Have they—have they *taken* him?" Her heart was in her voice.

Martin went across to her. "Only for questioning, and there's no need to worry. He's been in jams as bad as this before." He put a hand under her chin. There was the fresh loveliness of a young woman about Jessica which one often missed, because she was young—eighteen; but in spite of her *gamine* childhood, she looked younger. "Don't worry."

"Those ruddy cops!" she burst out.

"They're all right, Jessie. Don't worry."

" All *right*! " she echoed witheringly. " I hate them, every mother's son of them. Look at what they did to my dad. Never gave him a minute's peace, and now they're starting on you. And that beast had the *impudence* to ask me to go out with him one night ! "

Martin gaped. " Kelby ? "

" Oh, not *him*," said Jessica. " The sergeant. Wimple. Just because he's good-looking he thinks a girl will do anything. I told him where to get off."

" When was this ? "

" He looked in yesterday afternoon, said he'd come to see me, because he knew you weren't in," said Jessica. " I gave him a piece of my mind, all right."

" I'll bet you did," said Martin feelingly. He remembered the way Wimple had looked at the girl when he called with his semi-official message ; and he wondered whether Wimple had wanted to see her in the course of business, or whether he was attracted by her. " Jessie, I've an idea."

" Anything you say," said Jessie.

" Good girl. Next time Wimple asks you to go out with him—go."

" What ? " She was astounded, rebellious. " Go out with that—— "

" Wimple's a nice chap," interrupted Martin, " and he won't try any funny business. He might want to pump you about us. You needn't tell him anything that matters, but you can remember the questions he asks, and tell me about them afterwards. It might be useful."

Jessica hesitated before she conceded, " I suppose it might. Do you really want me to ? "

" Yes."

" Okay," said Jessica, almost wearily. " I don't know what the old man will say, though. I won't tell him until afterwards, and you'll have to stand by me. Say I was only obeying orders."

" Orders it is," said Martin gravely.

" Right you are." Jessica went back to her chair behind the reception desk.

As she sat down, unaware that she was being watched, Martin studied her. Would she attract Wimple ? She would attract a lot of men, but Wimple——

He gave it up, grateful that it had at least given him a diversion. Dwelling on Richard's plight wouldn't help. On the other hand, Richard was right not to want a lawyer at this stage; it would be much better if he could get through without one. Weighed up, this case had grown out of all proportion. It was a test case for the future of Prince, as well as for putting Richard on trial.

Barbara's door opened.

" All right, then," she said to June, " and telephone as soon as you can. Good-bye."

" I may take a few days," said June. " Good-bye. Good-bye, Mr. Fane." She went out briskly, smiling at Jessica; and Barbara, looking flushed because her room was too warm, laughed at Martin's expression.

" Richard isn't a fool," she said.

That cut like a knife. " No."

" And I like her. I should think she'll do what she's promised."

" What has she promised ? " Martin asked woodenly.

Barbara looked at him searchingly, read his anxiety, but didn't ask questions. She put a hand on his arm, and they went into his office. She sat on the corner of his desk.

" You hadn't briefed me, but I think I told her everything we'd like to find out—and how she might get hold of it."

Martin nodded.

" Richard's been taken to the Yard," he said abruptly.

Barbara slid off the table and went closer to him, but she didn't speak. He forced a grin.

" Better he than one of us," he said. " He always has the luck of the devil. It wouldn't surprise me if he comes back grinning all over his face, and saying that they've decided that he wouldn't do such a thing."

" Did they *know* he was there ? "

" Near enough. He was seen near by, and they heard of it. That means they had an anonymous phone call from one of the men who did the job. Richard came right out with it when he saw where things were heading. Best thing. We're doing nicely, aren't we ? Investigating murder for someone else and getting ourselves suspected and arrested. Not that he's under arrest—yet. Kelby was in his heaviest mood." Martin felt restless and talked jerkily. " We need to do something quickly, and I don't see how we can. I can even think that the police will wonder if we had anything to do with Hilda's death, too. As it happened at home."

"They're not utter fools," said Barbara.

"Meaning I am?" He forced a laugh, and tapped papers on his desk. "Look at these notes. We've tried everything, and come to a dead end. We haven't the faintest idea who the men were who killed Mrs. Grenfell. I actually saw Hilda's driver murdered in front of my eyes. Our one discovery is about Reginald Fraser's past, and none of us wants to believe he's a party to the murder." He stood up and paced the room. "Even if we know what's happening, we're going to have a hell of a job to prove it."

Barbara said, "*Do* you know?"

He looked at her sombrely. "No. Forget it. I do know two things. I'm going to have a look at Grenfell's place, and I'm going to find out what Rhoda knows about Hilda. They were such close friends that she might know something that will help. The police will be grilling her at Nairn Lodge, of course, but I don't think she'll respond well to police questions."

"Probably not," said Barbara, and went on soberly, "Scoop, hadn't you better hold your hand for a bit? Over Grenfell, I mean. It's sheer guesswork. I think June may pick up something, and if she finds any indication that Grenfell's in trouble, then you'll have something to work on. Don't be hasty. Whenever Richard's in a difficulty you seem to act more like him than yourself."

"I'll think about it," conceded Martin. He lit his pipe, and stood staring down at her. Two minutes passed before he smiled, went to her, and kissed her lightly. "I've thought! I'll go and see Grenfell over this new development—Hilda. Get his reaction. Any objection to that?"

"I suppose not," said Barbara.

She wasn't enthusiastic, probably because she was afraid that he would be too impetuous with Grenfell. He didn't try to re-assure her.

He telephoned Grenfell's office and learned that the newspaper owner was at his Langley Crescent home. Langley Crescent, in Mayfair, was within easy walking distance of Hilda Kennedy's flat.

He went out, drove to within a few yards of Grenfell's house, and then walked. He was admitted by a manservant who took his name and asked him to wait. Grenfell would probably dislike this direct approach; he would have to put up with it. It didn't occur to Martin that Grenfell would refuse to see him. He waited for five minutes, and began to feel restless. The room was small, obviously set aside for the less-important callers. A few magazines were on a polished walnut table, as they might be in a doctor's waiting-room.

Then the door opened, and June Grey came in.

Martin said, " Why, hallo ! " He didn't know why, but he had taken it for granted that June would work at the offices in Fleet Street. " Hallo," he added weakly.

June said quickly, " You do want to see him, don't you ? Not me."

" Oh, yes."

" I'm sorry," said June. " He says he can't possibly spare you any time, he's extremely busy. He *is* busy, too," she added, " but honestly, I think he'd rather not see you, just now. He'd see some people."

22   GRENFELL BACKS OUT

MARTIN had a feeling that June hadn't told him everything, was torn between eagerness to help and loyalty to her employer. She'd made it clear that Grenfell was shutting the door on him. He looked down at the carpet as he pondered, then glanced up and smiled.

" Where can I find him ? "

" Do you think you ought to go up ? "

" I'm going up," said Martin. " It would save time if I know the room, and don't go blundering."

" Turn right at the top of the stairs, and he's in the first room on the left of the small passage," said June. She had the gift of making up her mind quickly. " He's not in—a happy mood." She hesitated before using the word " happy ".

" You mean, he's in a foul temper ? "

"No, I wouldn't say that. Something's upset him, that's all. He's preoccupied and terse. I'm afraid you'll have a row if you break in."

"I'll risk it," said Martin. "Thanks. You'd better go up first, or he may suspect collaboration."

"I have to go into my office, next to his," said June. "He won't know that I haven't been there for some minutes." She turned and went out without looking back; she went up the stairs with a long-limbed grace which he couldn't fail to notice. He followed her more slowly, looking at the doors leading from the hall and the passage which ran alongside the stairs. No one appeared to be watching him. The thick carpet muffled the sound of his footsteps. He paused at the landing; three passages led off this, and one, on the right, was little more than a recess. No one was about up here, either. He went to the room June had described, tapped sharply, and went in.

Grenfell sat at a big, polished desk in a long, narrow room. The walls were panelled, the room had an atmosphere of luxury but not ostentation. Hide arm-chairs were dotted about, there was a radiogram, a television set, each in its own corner, and some black-and-white etchings and cartoons on the walls; probably original work of *Clarion* artists.

Grenfell had a pen in his hand and papers in front of him: pink slips; cheques. Glancing up, he presented a fore-shortened angle of his face, and for the first time Martin saw a likeness between him and Rhoda. He was dressed in a black coat, and probably striped grey trousers; he had a reputation for being correct.

He put the pen down and sat back slowly, his lips tightening.

"Sorry about this," said Martin. "I want to see you urgently." He went across to the desk, and Grenfell didn't speak. At closer quarters his eyes looked heavy, as if he had a severe headache or else hadn't slept well. His face was drawn, too. He looked through the cheques on his desk, selected one, signed it, and attached a letter to it. He handed these to Martin, all without a word.

Martin glanced down; the cheque was for £500 and made out to Prince. The letter read:

Dear Mr. Fane,

I have decided not to proceed with the investigation which I asked you to handle for me, and consequently will be glad if you will withdraw any of your operatives who may be working on it. In view of the short notice I am enclosing my cheque for £500.

Yours very truly

Edward Grenfell

Martin read this twice, glanced at the cheque, and felt a strong temptation to tear it up. He resisted, folded it slowly and deliberately, and put it in his pocket. Then he pulled up a chair and sat down.

" I'm sorry about that," he said. " I think we should have got results. But I'm not here as your agent. I'm investigating the death of Hilda Kennedy."

Grenfell's eyes sparked.

" Miss Kennedy died at my parents' home, and that gives me a close personal interest."

" I can tell you nothing to help."

" You could try," said Martin.

Grenfell said, " This is now a matter for the police. I don't intend to say anything to you or any one else except the police. I doubt if I can help them, but at least I can make it clear to you that I'll deal only with them. I'm extremely busy, Mr. Fane, as I'm sure my secretary told you."

" Oh, yes, she told me." Martin didn't get up. " So you know who's behind all this."

" I know nothing of the kind, and I don't intend to guess." Grenfell's fingers were drumming the desk. " I don't want to make myself unpleasant, but if you won't go I'll have to have you thrown out." He didn't smile ; he was serious.

" So you've strong-arm men," said Martin. " Can they shoot ? "

Grenfell jumped up, eyes blazing. " What the hell do you mean ? " He came close to Martin, his fists clenched.

" I mean that men of the chucker-out type killed your sister-in-law ; attacked me ; killed Hilda Kennedy's chauffeur. Do you know anything about it ? " Martin smiled nastily. " I'm just asking."

" Get out of here ! " cried Grenfell. He aimed a blow at

Martin's head.   Martin dodged it, sprang to his feet, gripped Grenfell's whirling arms and held them close to his sides, then actually lifted him clear of the floor and carried him back to his chair.   He dumped Grenfell into it, went back and sat down again.   His voice was quite calm.

"Why did you come to me in the first place?   Why didn't you use one of your own reporters?   They're better than I am.   You didn't mean to come at all, did you? You just followed Rhoda, and then tried to find out why she had called."

Grenfell, white to the lips, pressed a bell-push at the side of his desk.   He didn't speak.

Martin said, "Having me thrown out won't help.   If I tell the whole story to the Yard, they'll ask the same questions.   Why not keep me on your side?"

The door opened and a man came in; a man as tall as Martin, more heavily built, dressed discreetly in black, like a bruiser turned respectable.   He had an unexpectedly soft voice.

"Yes, sir?"

"Mr. Fane is overstaying his welcome," said Grenfell. "Show him out, Webber."

"Very good, sir."

Martin sat back, looking at the big man.   He could make a fight of it, and would probably lose; even winning wouldn't help.   There must be a way of making Grenfell change his mind, a way of shocking the man.   He got up, while the bruiser stood by politely, ready to act but not eager.   Martin went slowly to the door, his mind racing, one thought coming and being thrown out, another taking its place.   The bruiser went past him, and opened the door; actually bowed, from the waist.

He tried a shot in the dark.   "Who's been blackmailing you, Grenfell?" he asked.   "Do you want the police to know that story?"

The man in black raised his hands, and his eyes glinted, as if he were now eager to throw Martin out.   Martin didn't wait, but stepped into the recess.   He heard someone typing at a furious speed; it reminded him of his father, and he wondered what the Maestro would do in the same circumstances; probably the same thing, beat a retreat.   He reached the head of the stairs and started down, still walking slowly. He hadn't seen Grenfell's face after the mention of blackmail, but it looked as if the gambit had failed.

He reached the hall.

June called out from the landing, " Mr. Fane ! "

He turned. " Yes ? "

" Just a moment," said June. She hurried down. " Oh, Webber, Sir Edward would like to have a word with Mr. Fane, after all." Her manner with the servant was exactly right.

" Very well," said Webber, and looked disappointed as he followed them upstairs.

June didn't add another word, simply led the way to Grenfell's door, which was still open. Grenfell stood by the window, looking out into the street. He waited for the door to close on Martin before turning. The girl had gone. Grenfell looked pale, much more drawn, and his voice was taut.

" What have you discovered about blackmail ? "

Martin said, " It's at least part of the motive. Your sister-in-law suffered from it. I couldn't imagine you putting the inquiries out to an agency if it weren't a personal matter which you didn't want any of the *Clarion* staff to know. Blackmail was the most likely."

Grenfell said thinly, " So you're guessing."

" That's right," said Martin. " The police will guess, too. They've more facilities than I. They'll wonder who's blackmailing you—as I do. Now that Hilda Kennedy is dead, they'll have access to all her papers. They'll find that she was blackmailing you, and they'll remember that victims have often killed blackmailers. Won't they ? "

He hoped he was getting somewhere ; the words sounded empty enough, but in this new mood Grenfell might be persuaded to talk. There was a short silence—and then Grenfell began to smile, became the man who had been waiting in Martin's flat on the night of Rhoda's first visit. He went to his chair and sat down, still smiling ; he looked much happier, much more sure of himself.

" Now I know why Prince isn't making money," he said. " If you go on like this, it never will. So Hilda was black-mailing me, and I killed her. At least, I arranged that shooting in Dorset. Perhaps I had another motive, too—belief that she killed my sister-in-law. Or won't that fit in with your wonderful theories?" He laughed softly. "You'd better close up and find another job, Fane. You've been reading too many of your father's books. I needn't send for Webber this time, need I?"

Martin said, "All right. Why withdraw your inquiries?"

"They're no longer necessary."

"That's where we don't agree. Listen, Grenfell. I've a big personal interest in this now. I'm going to force the pace until I find the truth. I shan't stop because I might hurt you—or hurt anyone. You may think you're good enough to outsmart me and the police, but you'll find you're wrong. I'm giving you another chance, to tell me everything you know, to keep Prince on your pay-roll."

Grenfell's smile was derisive.

"Kind of you. I don't want your services, thanks."

Martin took the cheque out of his pocket, tore it in half, dropped the pieces on the desk, and said:

"I send you a bill for what you owe."

"And proud, too!" Grenfell marvelled. "There must be more in you than I've noticed yet. Do you need Webber to show you the door?"

Martin shrugged, and went out. He didn't feel proud of the way he'd handled the situation; the only remnant salvaged was the indication that Grenfell had been black-mailed; but Grenfell was quite sure that Hilda Kennedy hadn't been behind that. In Grenfell's change of manner, in his laughter after hearing the theory, there had been a significance it might be easy to overlook.

Martin walked downstairs, unaccompanied, and found a manservant standing by the door, ready to open it.

"Good afternoon, sir."

"'Afternoon," growled Martin.

It was nearly five o'clock, and getting dark. Cars passed with their lights on, and there were lights at many of the windows in the Crescent. He walked slowly to the car, feeling hot under the collar. Grenfell had virtually called him a young fool; he felt a young fool. He wallowed for five minutes in deep gloom; Prince had been a mistake, neither he nor Richard was cut out for this work, they were following a romantic idea, and the sooner they dropped it the better.

He laughed abruptly, as he turned into the Strand among dense traffic. Soon he was parked alongside Quill House. He sat at the wheel for a few minutes, trying to think of something he could do, instead of sit at the flat or office and twiddle his thumbs. Take Barbara out for the evening, for instance—that would be as much use as anything he'd tried so far. From the beginning he had been pushed around, and it was still happening. Two women had been murdered while he had been on the case, and he didn't know why.

He stiffened at the wheel.

He could waste a lot of time over the blackmail, which existed all right, but wasn't necessarily the motive. There was an angle no one had seen—or, at least, no one had mentioned it. The police were probably working on it now. The two murdered women had been intimate friends of Rhoda Grenfell. She hadn't many. Her earlier life had been full of acquaintances, until she had become serious and settled down. As far as he knew, she had had only three intimates : two dead, one alive.

Fraser was alive.

He started the engine and moved off, towards Covent Garden, taking a back way towards Mayfair and Fraser's flat. This was a Richard trick—acting on impulse, before weighing up all the relevant facts. Not that there were many to weigh ; two people dead, one alive——

He broke most of the traffic rules on his way, reached the mews, left the car in the narrow street outside, and hurried towards the flat. A single lamp glowed by a brick wall, and the window of the flat next to Fraser's showed as a yellow square. Radio music, rhythmic modern stuff, floated clearly over the cold night air. He started up the steps, and then noticed something glisten against the wall ; his own shadow hid most of it. He moved back two steps, and stared. A motor-cycle stood against the wall, facing the exit.

A motor-cycle ?

He went up slowly, and rang the bell ; there was no answer. He rang twice again, with the same result. He turned back and reached the ground, hesitated, then went straight to the exit. He was prepared to believe that he was making a fool of himself again. But the motor-cyclist who had tried to kill Hilda Kennedy might be in that flat, lying in wait for Fraser.

23 FRASER COMES HOME

MARTIN took the wheel of the Buick, drove to the next turning, swung round, and stopped a little way along. Then he hurried back to the entrance of the mews. He was taking long odds, but wasn't disposed to reject them. Two or three people walked along the gloomy street; there were few lights. Five cars passed, three from one direction, two from the other; none slowed down. He heard the plodding foot-steps of a policeman, not far away, and two women walked quickly beneath a lamp, garish make-up showing, high heels clicking. They didn't look at Martin.

Another car appeared, and slowed down. Martin stepped into the roadway, and heard Fraser call out:

"What's this? Suicide?"

Martin reached the window. "Let me get in, and drive on," he said.

"What's all this?" Fraser asked, but didn't argue. Martin got in, and instead of closing the door, held it so that it didn't swing open; thus, it didn't bang.

"First on the left," he said.

"What *is* this, Martin?" It was the first time Fraser had dropped the formal "Fane". Any danger that after his heart-searching story he would go into his shell seemed gone.

"Another crazy idea. Stop just behind my car, will you?"

Fraser stopped, and they sat in the darkness; Fraser took out cigarettes, and they lit up. Fraser waited; he had a lot of patience. Martin could see his teeth glistening as he smiled.

Martin said slowly, "I may be wrong, and probably am. But the man who killed Hilda Kennedy's driver escaped on a motor-cycle. There's one in the mews. Do motor-cycles often park in there?"

Fraser said, "Can't say I've seen one in weeks. Cars do."

"So no one near by owns a motor-cycle?"

"No. Chap could have decided it was a handy parking-place, though."

"If he did, fine, and we've nothing to worry about," said Martin. "If the long chance comes off, this chap may be waiting for you in the flat."

"My dear man! Not every one breaks in."

Martin said, "Let's go and see if the flat's empty, shall we? If it isn't, we can deal with the man and talk afterwards."

"We'll talk afterwards, anyhow," said Fraser. There was a hint of laughter in his voice. "Let's go. I haven't a gun—have you?"

"Yes," said Martin.

"Nothing's worth doing unless it's worth doing well." Fraser got out, and they walked towards the end of the street. "What's the plan of campaign?"

"Is there a back way in?"

"Not really. There's a way in from the roof at the back, but you have to be pretty agile to get up there. I did once, when I left my keys behind. Going to break in again?"

"Yes."

"Better let me. I know the way."

"Oh, no," said Martin. "You're to go to the front door when I'm about ready to get in through the roof. You can make a noise, pretend you've lost your key, say anything that can be heard inside the house. If the man's there, he'll be so interested in you that he won't think about a flank attack. Tell me how to get to the roof, and how long it should take to get through."

"Easy," said Fraser. "Five minutes."

"Now let's lower our voices," said Martin.

They were at the entrance to the mews, and walked through with little sound; certainly none that could be heard inside. Fraser probably thought that this was pure comedy, but at least he was backing up, and told Martin how to force entry. They passed the steps leading to the

flat. Twenty yards away was a window which had been
bricked-in ; the sill was still there, so was the sill of another
bricked-in window-space, immediately above.

"Up there," said Fraser. "Once you're on the roof,
pass the chimney-stack. It's easy until then. The roof-
light's on a slope. You'll have to lie full length, grip the
edge, and pull yourself up. I'm not so sure you can do it
without making some noise, but if you don't fall through, it
should be safe enough." Laughter was more noticeable in
his voice. "The roof-light works on hinges, and it's not
bolted on the inside—I've always kept it open for emergency. Think you'll be all right ? "

"Yes."

"I'll give you ten minutes, for safety."

Martin nodded, and climbed up to the first window-sill.
It was easy to get to the roof, and there was no danger
of being seen except from the mews. He stood upright for a
moment, then crouched and walked along, supporting himself against the chimney-stack. It was bitterly cold, and his
clothes made movement more difficult. There were stars,
and he was used to the darkness now and could make out the
outline of the roof-light. He faced it, lowered himself
gradually, and then stretched up, lying on his stomach and
with his feet resting against the channel between the sloping
roofs of the two adjoining flats. There was no danger of
falling. He touched the ledge of the roof-light, and hauled
himself up gradually, until his feet were free of the channel ;
that put all his weight on his arms. He took one hand away,
and groped, found a knob, and lifted ; the window opened
an inch, but the real danger lay in getting it wide open ; if he
just pushed it back, it would make a noise which would go
through the whole building.

He pulled himself up a foot. The slope wasn't steep,
there wasn't much risk of falling. It was easier than it had
looked. He pushed the roof-light back, and found that it
stayed erect, without being supported. Going head first
into the attic below wouldn't be much good. He manœuvred
until he could get his feet through, and made much more
noise than he liked.

He seemed to have been up here a long time ; had Fraser
allowed him long enough ?

He lowered his legs and touched the floor, while his head and shoulders were still above the roof-light. He took out a pencil torch and shone it round. Pale rafters showed up, and cobwebs hung down from the ceiling. A spider scuttled into a corner. A cistern gurgled. He saw the opening to the flat itself and stepped towards it cautiously, walking on rafters.

It opened easily—and the bathroom was below him.

He lowered himself, and had to drop a few inches; the thud seemed loud. He stood quite still, heart thumping. Then he rubbed his hands, for warmth. He was at the door before he remembered that this might be a fool's errand, there was no reason at all to think that any one was lying in wait for Fraser. Certainly Fraser didn't expect any one. If this proved futile, it would simply be following the general run of the case.

He heard a voice, some way off: Fraser's. He didn't catch the words. He opened the bathroom door. As he had seen on his earlier visit, this led into the kitchen, and the kitchen-door opened into the small passage coming from the front door. He put out the torch and stepped cautiously across the kitchen, feeling foolish; it wouldn't take much to make him call out to Fraser, who was talking to himself, and words came through faintly:

" I know I had that damned key ! Where is it ? "

Silence followed.

Martin peered into the hall. Some light shone through the fanlight, from the mews.

A small man stood close to the front door, back to Martin, right hand in his pocket, left hand stretched out to pull open the door. He didn't touch the door-handle until he had taken his right hand from his pocket.

He had a gun.

.   .   .   .   .

Martin stared at the little man incredulously; now that it had happened, he could hardly believe it. Then he saw the left hand touch the door knob. He stepped forward swiftly, softly, and the man turned the knob. He was going to pull it sharply, and shoot.

Martin gripped him by the nape of the neck and by the

right forearm. He gasped, dumbfounded, tried to slew round, then cried out as Martin twisted his arm. The gun dropped. Martin kicked it away, held the right wrist in a grip which the man couldn't loosen, and opened the door.

" Come in," he said, and switched on the light.

* * * * *

It was the best moment of the case so far. The door opened wide, Fraser moved forward, grinning; and the grin froze on his face. The little man squirmed, but was helpless. Fraser gulped and came forward, closed the door and leaned against it. He gulped again.

" Well, well," he said weakly. " Not a bad guess. You didn't put him here just to impress me with your omniscience, did you ? "

" Pick up his gun," said Martin.

Fraser looked about him. " Gun," he echoed inanely. " Why, so there is. All as you expected." He picked up the gun and stared at it. " Ugly-looking thing. Lethal, too. Think he was going to shoot me ? "

" No ! " gasped the little man. " No, I wasn't, I wasn't going to shoot you ! "

" Considerate of you," said Fraser. " Let's take him into the sitting-room and make him comfortable, shall we ? " He opened the door opposite the kitchen, and Martin pushed his captive in. Fraser took out a handkerchief and dusted the seat of a chair. " Sit down," he invited.

" Hold him a minute," said Martin.

Fraser obeyed. Martin ran his hands over the man, felt something hard at his waist, undid his waistcoat, and found a knife; a long, thin, sheathed knife. He held it gingerly, and put it on a table. The man moistened his lips. Martin made sure there were no other weapons, then emptied the man's pockets and put everything by the side of the knife. Finished, he pushed the man into the chair; he collapsed, as if he were made of rubber.

" Martin," said Fraser, in a curiously unsteady voice. " Thanks."

" Forget it."

" Think you could do with a drink ? " asked Fraser. " I know I can't do without one." Reaction had set in, as he went to a cupboard and took out whisky and soda, while Martin looked down at the prisoner. He was pretty sure that he had seen the man before. He picked up his hat and put it on his head, then pushed it back—as the branch of a tree had pushed back the hat of the man who had killed the chauffeur.

This was the same man.

. . . . .

Fraser came over with the drinks, said, " Cheers," and tossed down whisky, which was hardly diluted with soda. Martin sipped his, and handed back the glass. Fraser took it without a word, went to the cupboard and squirted in more soda. He came across again, looking at the little man, whose eyes were almost popping out of his head. He had a thin, narrow face and eyes that were almost black, dark hair, oiled heavily and brushed straight back from his low forehead. He wore a heavy blue Melton belted coat, now open, and a blue suit and brown shoes; all the clothes were of good quality.

Martin had another drink, while looking through the contents of the man's pocket. Fraser, waiting for his cue, didn't speak. The victim looked from one to the other, started to speak, stopped himself, and then muttered something under his breath. As Martin examined a letter addressed to Claude Morris, with an address in Clerkenwell, he burst out:

" I wasn't going to shoot him ! "

Neither of the others spoke. Martin found a driving-licence, also in the name of Claude Morris, and several other papers. There were stamps, twenty pound notes and several ten-shilling notes, and the photograph of a blonde girl who looked more pert than pretty, and who favoured the Edwardian hair style.

" I wasn't ! " gasped Claude Morris.

Martin finished his inspection, left everything on the table except the knife, and examined that thoughtfully. Fraser came across to him.

" Nasty-looking weapon."

" Yes." Martin pointed to the join between blade and handle. " See that."

" Brown mark, you mean ? "

" Blood."

" No ! " exclaimed Fraser.

The little man started up from his chair. " It isn't blood, you're wrong ! And I wasn't going to shoot—— "

Martin stretched out his arm, pressed the flat of his hand against the man's chest, and pushed him back into the chair. He went down more like rubber than ever, and stared, with his frightened eyes switching from one man to the other.

" It's blood, all right," Martin said. " Mrs. Grenfell's, probably. She was killed with a long knife, like this. I should say it's the same one."

" It isn't ! " screamed the little man. "It can't be ! I didn't kill her ! I wasn't going to shoot ! "

Neither of the others took any notice, and his voice trailed off. Martin took the gun which Fraser still had in his hand, looked at it thoughtfully, and nodded.

" A point three two. The driver of Hilda Kennedy's car was shot with one of these. Probably the same gun. It looks as if we've found a killer, doesn't it ? The motorcycle clinches it—I'm pretty sure it's the same one. We'll soon be able to find out, anyhow. The police can check the bullets from this, too, and the blood with Mrs. Grenfell's blood group. It'll all tie up. We haven't much farther to look."

" Fair cop," Fraser said ; he had fully recovered.

" It's not true ! " cried the little man. He struggled to get up again, but didn't stand. " I didn't shoot any one, didn't knife anyone, it isn't my motor-bike, it—— "

Martin turned and looked at him for the first time ; and he broke off. He licked his lips and cringed back in his chair. Martin weighed the gun in his hand as he looked, was silent for a moment, and then said very slowly :

" You've had it, Morris. You're the killer. I feel sorry for you. You were paid to do it, but money won't help you when you're on the gallows, will it ? "

Morris gasped : " I—didn't—— " and couldn't go on.

" Why waste your breath ? " asked Martin. " I can bring the police, and within an hour or two they'll have all the evidence they need to hang you. Of course, I needn't send for the police. If you'll talk—— "

He stopped, and waited.

24

GIVE AWAY

MORRIS was so terrified that he might fall for that; might believe that he would be given a chance to escape. His eyes darted to and fro, Fraser kept a blank face, Martin thrust his hands in his pockets and looked as if he couldn't care less.

" What—what do you want ? " Morris muttered.

" I told you I felt sorry for you," said Martin. " You're not in this alone, you just have to do the dirty work. You were at Mrs. Grenfell's flat the other night, with someone else. And there was almost certainly someone with you in Dorset. You attacked me at my flat, too—with a second man, a bigger chap than you. You stick your neck out, and he keeps his in. Why stand for that ? "

Morris didn't speak.

" Who is he ? " Martin asked evenly.

Morris said thinly, " I—I dunno."

Martin guessed the torment of his mind. The first flare of hope had died, he knew that there was no real hope of getting away, so—he wouldn't talk. There *was* honour among thieves. He might talk to the police, but not for a while.

The full implications of this were showing now; with luck, the knife would free Richard from all suspicion. The police would have to know soon, but—this was a Prince investigation. If Martin learned the whole story he would force Kelby to show greater respect, would establish Prince once and for all.

He said, " Look here, Morris, you've had a raw deal." In fact, Morris deserved no one's sympathy, was a hired killer; but playing on his sympathy now might work. " Now you're caught, you'll be stranded. Think the man who employs you will care if you get hanged ? Not on your life ! Why should he ? Will he worry about your wife ? " He went across to the table and picked up the photograph; and reflected that there was no proof that Morris was married or that this was his wife.

Morris didn't speak, didn't deny anything.

" I can look after her," Martin said. " And I can help

you, even if the police catch up with you. King's evidence might save you from the gallows, anyhow. Tell me who employs you. I'll go and see him, leaving you here. When I've found out everything, I'll give you a break, if I can. In any case, we'll have every one, you won't have to stand the rap alone. I'm working with the police on this job, anyhow."

Was that going too far ?

Morris muttered, " How do I know I can believe you ? "

Martin shrugged. " You have to take the chance. Of course, you can say no. Then I'll have to get tough." He gave a short bark of a laugh. " I feel sorry for you, I don't want to knock you about, but I'll knock the truth out of you somehow. And if I have to get tough, I won't put a word in for you. You won't stand a chance of turning King's Evidence—the police will have all the evidence they need without you. Please yourself."

He turned to Fraser.

Fraser shrugged his shoulders. " Your job," he said. " I'll just look on. Don't go too far, I remember that man you dealt with at—— " He paused, then grinned. " Staines. Lord, what a mess he was when you finished with him."

Martin said carelessly, " That was nothing."

Until that moment he had been on top of the world ; now, without warning, his mood changed. He couldn't explain it, but he felt uneasy. He glanced round, not because he thought that anyone else was here——

The door was opening.

His expression changed, he swung round, gun in hand— but before he reached the door it opened wide. A man with a scarf over his face appeared for a split second, and fired three times. The shots roared. Morris screamed. Martin fired twice, but the door slammed and the key turned.

.   .   .   .   .

" Window ! " roared Fraser.

He rushed to the window, but it was latched. The gun-man was running down the outside steps. Morris was moaning. Fraser swore, flung the window up, and then heard the first staccato beat of a motor-cycle engine. Martin reached Fraser's side, but they couldn't see the cyclist. The engine roared, then snorted as it moved towards the exit.

Martin fired.

The motor-cycle roared out of the mews and along the street.

.   .   .   .   .

Morris was slumped in his chair. There was blood on his face, dripping from a wound in his forehead; not a serious wound. There was blood on his hand, too. He was staring down at it, stupidly. It had come from his chest—he had pulled his coat aside, and showed the red patch spreading over his shirt. It might be too high for real danger. Martin had forced the lock, and the door was open.

" Get some blankets, put a kettle on, and fetch water and a towel, will you ? " He went to Morris, moved the coat aside, and unbuttoned the man's shirt. He could see the wound high on the left side; too high for the heart, but the bullet might have touched the lung. Morris had lost his colour, and his face was puckered in pain.

Martin said slowly, " Now you know what you can expect from your friends. Rather than have you caught, he tried to kill. Who was he ? "

Morris closed his eyes.

" Who was he ? " Martin insisted.

Morris caught his breath, gasped with pain, opened his eyes, and looked frightened, as if he knew that death was in the background.

" Slippy Lee," he muttered. " Slippy Lee, you'll find him at the Lion, Wapping. The swine! The swine, he—he tried to *kill* me." He sounded absurdly naïve; astonished.

" That's right," said Martin.

Fraser came in with the blankets; Martin put them round Morris, and Fraser went in to fill a hot-water bottle; all treatment for shock. Then Martin started first aid—the only useful thing he could do now was pad the wound. He didn't want to move Morris, laid him flat, with high-back chairs placed in front of the other, like a couch. He worked quickly.

Fraser was telephoning for a doctor.

Martin called, " Better make it the police. Ask for Sergeant Wimple."

" Right."

Morris had closed his eyes again, and showed no sign that he had heard. Martin padded the wound and stemmed the bleeding, then straightened up. Fraser was already talking to Wimple. He finished, rang off, and Martin lifted the receiver and dialled the office number. As he waited for an answer, he said to Fraser :

" Still in this ? "

" Believe me, I'm still in it," said Fraser heavily.

Martin was ponderous.

" I'm going to tackle Slippy Lee myself. Morris won't be able to talk to the police for a while. I doubt if he'll come round. I'd like to find Lee and make him talk, but—— "

" I know," said Fraser. " Danger. Who cares ? "

Barbara's voice sounded on the line, clear, refreshing. " This is Prince."

Martin said, " Hallo, my sweet. I want—— "

" Scoop ! " Barbara's voice became loud, he thought that she was excited; and next moment, knew why. " Richard's back ! They haven't held him, Kelby just read him the Riot Act. Of course, it may be a trick, but they can't seriously suspect that he killed Mrs. Grenfell."

" Hear, hear." That was Richard, on the extension. " Only a very light stain on my character so far, Scoop, and I'm as free as the air."

" Good." Martin was so intense that he hardly noticed his relief, and his voice wasn't enthusiastic. " Listen. Meet me at Aldgate Pump in half an hour. It's urgent. Barbara—— "

" Yes ? " All her excitement had gone, she was anxious.

" If I haven't called again by half-past seven, get in touch with the Yard and tell them they want a man named Slippy Lee, who stays at the Lion, Wapping. 'Bye, my sweet."

He rang off.

Fraser was already at the door, and had Morris's gun in his gloved hand. Martin took it from him, without a word, and tossed it on to a chair. Morris was unconscious;

he looked waxen pale. The two men hurried out, and Fraser was about to slam the door. Martin put a foot against it.

" The police will want to get in," he said.

" Sorry."

" We must look slippy," said Martin. " They'll have a patrol car here in a few minutes. We'll use your car—they know mine too well."

" Right."

They half-ran towards the street where the cars were parked. Two or three people were standing about; obviously the shot from the window had been heard. No one tried to stop them. They reached Fraser's car, a Jaguar, and the engine started at a touch. Fraser drove off, and Martin sat back, relaxing for the first time since he had thought Fraser might be in danger; and realised a possible common denominator. Yet he couldn't afford to relax. Fraser was somehow involved, or wouldn't have been a subject for murder; nothing in his story explained why he had been attacked. He was still an unknown quantity.

Fraser said, " Back way to Aldgate Pump ? "

" I don't think the back way matters yet. Get there fast."

" All right. Now you've a spare minute, why did you pull this stunt to-night ? What made you think I might be next on the list ? " Fraser took his eyes off the road for a moment. " I didn't give it a thought. I can't say I'm elated about it, it might give you ideas."

" Not about you," Martin said slowly. He meant it.

" Explain, please."

" Not now," said Martin. " There's a lot to do, and I don't want to be side-tracked."

Fraser drove on for a few minutes in silence, and then said heavily :

" Meaning, I shan't like what you can tell me."

" I don't know. Forget it," said Martin. He stared ahead of him as they went past St. Paul's, the great dome blotting out a patch of sky and stars. On either side were the open spaces where once there had been buildings and offices, and where wild flowers and grass now grew ; this was the part of London that had died during the war, and had not come to life again. They passed the Bank and went along Leadenhall Street. The grey buildings of the City showed up in the street-lamps, but few people were about. There was little traffic on the narrow streets, but now and again they passed a bus, which looked like a monstrous, fiery-eyed leviathan. The kerbs sparkled with frost. Soon they came to Aldgate Pump, which stood on a corner which had once marked the limits of London in the east.

There was no sign of Richard.

"What's the plan?" asked Fraser, making no attempt to re-open the other subject.

"We'll have a look round the pub first," said Martin. "You or Richard can ask for Slippy Lee, and the other will come with me—there'll be a side entrance. I fancy he lives over the pub, Morris didn't mean that he would be there for a drink."

"No. And then?"

"Find out who employs him."

"He won't be as easy as Morris."

"Won't he?" asked Martin softly.

Fraser didn't speak.

A taxi pulled up just behind them. Richard jumped out, paid the cabby off quickly, and came running; he seemed to have recovered completely. He climbed into the back of the car and leaned forward over the seats. Martin looked round, as Fraser started off, and told him about Morris. Richard listened intently, and made little comment.

"Know your way?" Martin asked Fraser.

"I can find Wapping."

"Mis-spent youth," said Richard. "Well, we are going places, aren't we? For ever after I shall cease to claim that I'm the only man in the family with a brilliant mind. What put you on to it, Scoop?"

Martin said, "You know as much as I do. Well, nearly as much." He told them about Grenfell briefly, then fell silent. He didn't want to talk, he wanted to let things slide through his mind easily—all the things that had happened, the debit and the credit.

There was no longer any need to worry about Richard. The police might give a slap or two for this chase after Slippy Lee, but wouldn't have many grounds for complaint, now that Morris had been handed over to them. The knife and the gun would make their case against Morris, but that wasn't the whole case.

They were in the mean, dimly lit streets of the East End. Trams clattered. Small shops on either side were closed, lights showed only at the pubs and the billiard saloons and, here and there, at a church and at windows in flats above the shops. Fraser obviously knew the district well, and turned off the main road through a narrow street where the houses opened straight on to the pavement. Although it was so cold, children played football in lamplight, one ran wildly in front of the car, screaming with laughter as Fraser jammed on his brakes.

They reached the end of the street, and a policeman turned the corner.

" He'll know," said Richard.

" Shall we ask him ? " Fraser spoke cautiously.

" Might as well."

The policeman was incurious, gave them directions to the Lion, and didn't stand and watch as they drove off. The directions were easy to follow, and twenty minutes after leaving Aldgate they saw the pub.

It was the one really bright spot in the district. Lights blazed from windows on the ground floor and upstairs. Men were standing outside, and the doors opened and closed several times as the car approached. Men who had been talking stopped and looked at the car as it slowed down. Fraser drew up just beyond it, and all three climbed out. Fraser slipped the key into his pocket. As they neared the main door the smell of beer reached them.

Martin passed a doorway, probably the side door. A light was on immediately above it. He and Richard stayed near the door. Two men at the corner could see them, but Martin wasn't worried about the Lion's ordinary customers. Fraser went into the pub ; the watching men turned their attention to him.

Martin tried the side door.

" Locked ? " whispered Richard.

" Yes."

" Let me fix it."

He was slicker at the job than Martin. Martin stood aside

as Richard worked with a skeleton key, and after a moment or two stood back.

" You first," he said.

" We'll wait for Fraser," Martin said.

25   NO SLIPPY

THEY stood waiting, Richard tapping his foot up and down on the pavement, Martin quite still. He wasn't sure that these tactics were right. He hadn't given this approach enough thought, partly because he had been so anxious to get here ahead of the police. Morris might come round soon. That wasn't the only reason; he had been preoccupied about Fraser and the reason for his own impulse to go to the mews. He liked Fraser; the liking might be dangerous.

Fraser appeared.

" Well ? " asked Richard in a hoarse whisper.

" They say he used to live here," said Fraser quietly. " I'm not sure we handled it the right way. They'd lie like troopers to stop us from getting him, wouldn't they ? "

Martin said, " I've been thinking that, but work it out. What else could we have done ? " He'd reached that thought himself, but it wasn't comforting. " One of you two stay here, will you ? "

" *Must* I ? " asked Fraser.

Richard said unexpectedly, " I'll be dummy." He probably thought trouble more likely to come from outside.

Martin opened the door, and stepped into a dark passage. Fraser followed, close on his heels. The door closed. By now, word would almost certainly have been passed on to the men inside the pub, and if Lee were here he would expect them. Martin kept a tight hold on his gun as he went upstairs. A faint light shone from there, and the smell of beer persisted. He reached a small landing. The light came from a door, standing ajar, on his right. There were two other doors. Martin opened each, found a bathroom and a bedroom, both empty. No sound came from the room with the open door. Fraser kept close to him, but did not attempt to go anywhere first.

Martin touched the door.

Someone hiccoughed.

He opened the door wider, and saw a small room, furnished plainly but neatly. There was a couch on one side, and a woman lay on it, shoes off, hair disarranged; a blonde who had a lot of hair—a lot of everything. She stared blankly at them, and hiccoughed again. Her face was red and her eyes were bleary; she looked drunk—or she was acting drunk. A bottle of gin stood on a small table by her side.

She blinked as Martin went in.

When Fraser followed, she fluttered her eyelids, and struggled up to a sitting position. She swayed, and stretched out a hand to the bottle, and grinned.

" Hallo, pal," she said.

" Hallo," said Martin. " How are tricks ? "

" Lovely, ducks. I'm 'aving a *lovely* time. See that ? " She raised the bottle. " My second—hic !—to-night. 'Ave a little drink ? "

" Thanks."

She fumbled beneath the table and brought out a second glass. Her hand wasn't steady. Martin took the bottle and poured, and she clapped her hands with delight. He backed away.

" Where's Slippy ? " he asked casually.

" Don't you talk to me about Slippy." She wagged a finger. " Left me 'igh and dry, 'e did. We was going out to-night, and what 'appens ? Left me 'igh an'—dry. Hic ! " She giggled. " Not so dry ! I got my methods. Drink up, pal."

Martin sipped ; the neat gin nauseated him.

" Where's he gone ? "

Her eyes narrowed cunningly. " You're not a copper, are you ? "

" No, I'm not a copper, I'm just a friend who wants to talk to Slippy."

" *Friend ?* "

Martin grinned. " Say a business associate."

" That's diff'rent," she said owlishly. " I can't imagine a gentleman like you being a friend of Slippy. Hic ! Dirty

tyke. Left me 'igh!" She giggled again. " 'E's gone to
see another—bushness associate!"

She burst into a loud laugh, pressed her hand deeply into
her breast as if she couldn't hold her breath, and began to
splutter and cough. She went purple in the face, and the
paroxysm lasted for a long time. When she recovered, she
lay back, panting.

Martin poured her out another drink.

"Ta, ducks. You're a sport, you are. Know what
Slippy says? Says I drink too much! I'll show 'im." She
drank half the gin.

"Where is he?" asked Martin.

She waved a hand, making a complete circle, drank more
gin, and then beckoned him, although he was standing only
two feet away. He bent down, getting nearer. She took
his head between her hands, turned it a little, and put her
lips close to his ear.

"Do you really want to know?"

"Yes."

"Don't tell no one," she said. "Don't tell Slippy I told
you. Wouldn't 'arf 'ave it in for me, 'e would, if 'e knoo I'd
told you. Gone to see a very fine gentleman. Lives in
Mayfair. Got a title, too." She pushed him away, and
giggled. "What do you think o' *that*?"

Martin said slowly, "What's the man's name?"

She thrust her head forward, eyes wide open, lips pursed,
and then she wagged her forefinger.

"Gre'fell," she said. "Sir So-and-so Ruddy Gre'fell.
Teddy Gre'fell. That's 'oo. Don't tell Slippy!" She sat
up again, and looked anxious, almost frightened. " 'E'd
cut my froat if——"

"I won't tell him," said Martin. He watched her finish
her drink, poured her out another, left his own glass near,
hardly touched, and went out. Fraser was already on the
landing. They went downstairs quietly.

It had been so easy that the snag must be waiting for them.
Fraser voiced that thought in a whisper. Martin grunted.

Richard stood near the door, visible against the light from
the glass panels.

"All clear," he said. "Get anything?"

"We got everything we wanted," Fraser said with a note

of restrained jubilation. " Slippy Lee's lady-friend was tight and resentful. He's gone to see a real gent. A titled gent."

" Grenfell," Richard said softly.

" None other. What are you waiting for, Martin ? "

Martin was standing by the door and looking up and down; the light showed his frown, which suggested that he was puzzled, dissatisfied. Fraser shrugged, and went to the car. Two urchins were gaping at it, one breathing on the black cellulose.

" Give us a ride, guv'nor."

" Some other time," said Fraser absently.

The Fanes were together, but he didn't think they were talking. He sat at the wheel and switched on the engine. The Fanes came up, and Richard got into the back. Martin had hardly closed his door before the car moved off.

" Grenfell's place ? " asked Fraser.

" Nearest telephone first, please."

Richard exploded from the back. " Must you be a Sphinx ? You've got it straight, haven't you ? "

" I don't like it," said Martin slowly. " It was too easy. Was she drunk or acting drunk ? Would a man with the resource of Slippy Lee let us get away with it as easily as that ? It looked almost as if we were expected."

Fraser grunted.

Richard said, " You imagine too much."

They neared a corner, and a light glowed in a telephone kiosk. Fraser stopped. Martin streaked to the box, and once inside, held the door ajar with his foot, putting the light out. He peered up and down the street, but saw no sign of a car approaching without lights, nothing to suggest that they had been followed. He dropped two pennies into the box, and dialled Grenfell's number. Outside, Richard and Fraser lit cigarettes, and the match or lighter brightened the inside of the car.

The number was ringing. Brrr-brrr—brrr-brrr.

It stopped.

" This is Sir Edward Grenfell's house." The voice was June's, clear and immediately recognisable.

Martin said, " June, listen. This is Martin Fane, and I want to talk to him. Is he there ? "

"Yes, but——"

"I can guess his mood," said Martin. "I still have to talk to him. Is he alone?"

"Yes."

"Has he had any callers to-night?"

"No visitors, but several people have telephoned. I don't know all of them, he had the 'phone switched through to his room for half an hour."

"All right. Now put me through to him, will you? I know he'll probably dress you down for doing it, but take the risk. This is really urgent."

"All right," she said crisply.

He heard the sound of the connection being made, then Grenfell's voice, low-pitched, tired. Martin had been casting round for something to make sure that Grenfell wouldn't ring off; and he thought he had it. He said:

"I've just been told that the men who killed Mrs. Grenfell worked for you, Grenfell. I don't believe it—yet."

Grenfell caught his breath, and the sound seemed loud. Then he said sharply:

"Who? Oh—Fane."

"I want to talk to you. If this evidence reaches the police, you'll have a lot of trouble getting out of it."

Grenfell said slowly, "Another guess?"

"The man who killed your sister-in-law and the man who killed Hilda Kennedy's chauffeur is in hospital, under police supervision," said Martin. "I caught him this afternoon. Don't make any mistake this time."

"*You* caught him?"

"That's right."

Grenfell said, "Come round."

"I'll be there in half an hour. Listen to me. Stay in your room. Don't go outside. If you do, you might catch more than you expect. Can you trust your secretary?"

"June Grey? Yes, she—damn it, Fane, what are you talking about?"

Martin said, "You could be next on the list."

He rang off, looked up and down again before stepping out of the kiosk and into the car. Richard greeted him with a subdued, "Howdy, Sphinx?"

Martin grunted as Fraser drove off. He waited until they had reached the main road, and then said quietly :

" Show me where I'm wrong, will you ? Two people, who were intimates of Rhoda Grenfell, have died. A third would have been dead this afternoon, but for a big slice of luck. There's only one man left who could be called an intimate— who might know a lot about Rhoda, who might be able to influence her to take a certain course of action. That's Grenfell."

Richard whistled ; Fraser didn't speak.

" Now knock holes in this," said Martin. " Slippy Lee shot Morris at the flat—we've taken that for granted and there isn't much doubt. He was there, keeping watch on the mews, realised things had gone wrong, and probably got in the same way as I did. He shot, but couldn't be sure he'd killed Morris. He'd allow for Morris saying something before he died—for naming him. So he would assume that we might find out all about the Lion."

" Go on," said Richard.

" And he would have things laid on at the Lion," said Martin. " A reception party. A woman who pretended to be drunk and annoyed with him, who'd give him away. That was a plant, if I've ever seen one. She named Grenfell —because Slippy wanted Grenfell named. He told her how to act, what to do. Grenfell is obviously in line for murder. If we go there now, not to protect or warn him, but thinking he is the real killer—— "

Fraser said, " I wish I didn't, but I think you're right. Go on."

" Slippy Lee probably has an idea that Morris talked some more. He knows we've been working on the job, doesn't know what Hilda or Rhoda told us. In other words, we could know a lot he doesn't want us to pass on. Knowing we'll want to do this job ourselves, he can be sure that we'll go to Grenfell's place and not the police. We can assume that he wants to kill Grenfell. If we think Grenfell's behind the murders we shan't be on his side. That will make it nice and easy for Slippy, who will be glad to see the Fane brothers on their way out, too. Three birds with one stone, so to speak. Or four, with Fraser. The only flaw is that we've spotted the plant, and we aren't going after

Grenfell." He lit a cigarette. " Yes, I know it's all guess-work."

" My money's on it," Richard said. " How many guns have we got between us ? "

" You carrying one ? "

" Yes."

" Then we've two."

" Call it three," said Fraser dryly. " I slipped one in my pocket after the show at the flat. I don't mind being shot at if I can shoot back. What's the drill ? "

Doubts about Fraser couldn't be kept out; but if Fraser were involved, the only way to protect themselves against him was by watching him.

Martin said slowly, " There isn't a back way. There's a semi-basement with a basement approach from that front, that's all. There are windows at the back, but I wouldn't like to get in that way. It could happen in the street, but I think it's much more likely to happen when we're inside the house. So I'm going in."

" *We're* going in," Richard said. " No stooge duty this time, chaps."

Martin said, " Let's get it straight. Sure you're in this gamble, Fraser ? "

" Yes."

" Then we'll have the Fane risk," Martin said. " As soon as we're in the West End, I'll get a taxi and go straight there. Ten minutes later, you get a taxi and follow me. We'll both go up to the front door and get in the usual way— if we can. Richard will drive up, ten minutes after that. If neither you nor I are giving the all-safe sign, he'll fetch the police."

Fraser would be sandwiched between them, that way; all that was now needed was a warning to Richard of the possibility of danger from the other man; Richard probably didn't need telling.

Fraser said, " You could send for the police first. Any strong reason why you don't want to ? " When Martin didn't answer, he went on, " Prince will come out of this with honours, it can't simply be that. What is it ? "

Doubts of him almost faded.

" I think we might stop another killing this way," said

Martin. " It's worth trying." Fraser started the engine, and Richard hung back.

" Watch *him*," Martin said softly.

" I'm watching every one." Richard got in, and Fraser drove off.

26 FAMILY QUARREL

MARTIN paid his taxi off at the corner of the crescent, and walked briskly towards Grenfell's house. Two people strolled along on the opposite pavement, and passed beneath a lamp; man and woman, intent on each other. No one appeared to be interested in Grenfell's house, no one was hiding in the nearby porches.

The area in front of each house here was approached by a flight of stone steps, and each made a good hiding-place. Martin opened the iron gate leading to the steps of Grenfell's house, and went half-way down. No one was there. He returned, closed the gate, and went to the front door.

He rang the bell, and after a pause there came a muffled sound; as of a door banging. Then a man approached, the door opened and showed a small light in the hall.

" Good evening, sir." It was Webber, the strong-arm man.

" Is Sir Edward in ? "

" Yes, sir, and expecting you." The manservant stood aside, and Martin went in. The door closed behind him softly. He glanced round; everything seemed to be normal. He followed the manservant up the stairs. A light shone on the landing. He found himself smiling grimly as the man tapped on Grenfell's door, and Grenfell called :

" Come in."

The room was exactly as Martin had seen it before, except that Grenfell sat in one of the arm-chairs, with a whisky-and-soda by his side; and June Grey stood near him, with a glass in her hand. Grenfell stood up slowly; and the sardonic smile on his lips wasn't encouraging.

" You've kept one promise, anyhow," he said. " You're here. I wish you wouldn't spread so much alarm, Fane."

"There's plenty of time to justify alarm," said Martin.

"More ominous hints." Grenfell turned to a cocktail cabinet. "Have a drink, and tell me all about it. I can't imagine being in personal danger."

"Can't you?" Martin looked from the man to the girl.

Grenfell was in a much happier mood than he had been; that was puzzling. June's eyes were sparkling, there was a touch of radiance to her calm loveliness. Was she part of the explanation of Grenfell's new mood?

"Can you prove your case?" asked Grenfell.

"Not yet," said Martin.

"Who told you this nonsense about working for me?"

"Listen," said Martin. "I've found the murderer. He's trying to persuade people that you employ him. I think it's a lie."

Grenfell laughed. "But make the proviso that it could be true! Fane, sit down, drink up, and listen. There are several things I can freely tell you now—I couldn't, a few hours ago. First—"

He stopped abruptly.

He had sharp ears, for he heard the running footsteps before Martin. He frowned as he looked towards the door. Then it burst open, and Rhoda came in, breathing heavily, cheeks flushed, eyes blazing. She didn't close the door but approached Grenfell, who was getting out of his chair. She stood a yard away from him, and she looked at her best. She didn't appear to notice Martin or June. Her voice was husky with emotion which she tried to keep back.

"You killed them," she said.

Grenfell didn't speak.

"You killed them," Rhoda went on in the same husky voice. "You killed mother and Hilda. I know, now. And I know why. You thought they were blackmailing you. You thought they knew about your miserable past. So you hired thugs to kill them. I *know*. The man who did it for you told me, I paid him a fortune for the truth. I'm going to make sure the police find out."

Grenfell said quietly, "Take it easy, Rhoda. I don't know what man's been filling you up with lies—"

"Lies? It's the truth!" She took her hands out of

the big pockets of her tweed coat. "You swine. You *devil*.
I ought to kill you myself!"

June took a half-step towards her.

Rhoda snapped, "Don't you come near me!"

Martin, sideways to her, kept quite still, except for
dropping his hand to his pocket and gripping his gun.

"Rhoda——" began Grenfell.

"It's no use talking," she said. "I wish I could kill you,
make you suffer. I——"

"By the way," said Martin unexpectedly, "how did you
get in?"

Grenfell said, "She has a key." Outwardly, he was quite
calm. "Rhoda, you've lost your senses. This man, whoever he is, lied to you. Fane knows that. Don't you,
Fane?"

"Oh, yes," said Martin. "He's a liar, no doubt at all."
He sounded casual, and Grenfell looked at him in surprise.
"The trouble will be to prove it." Martin kept glancing
towards the door, and went on easily, "How much did you
pay him, Rhoda?"

"I paid him enough!" Rhoda spat. "More than
enough to——"

Martin saw the door open, watched the handle tensely,
saw a hand. He slewed round. The girl broke off. A man
appeared for a split second in the doorway, his gun showing.
Grenfell fell sideways as a shot rang out. Martin fired. His
bullet thudded against the steel of the other's gun. Martin
leapt, seeing June rush rowards Grenfell.

Rhoda screamed, "Stop him!"

Martin beat her to the door. A shot rang out, but he
felt nothing. On the landing a man was running towards
the stairs. Martin fired again, aiming low, and saw the man
pitch forward, then fall out of sight. Martin paused at the
top of the stairs, with Rhoda behind him, and saw the man
half-way down; the gun still in his hand.

He fired.

Martin felt the bullet pluck at his left arm, flinched, and
fired again as he dodged to one side. He didn't want to kill.
He heard a shout from somewhere downstairs, and a cry
from behind him.

"Martin! He's been hit—he's hurt!"

"I'm glad," cried Rhoda wildly. "He murdered the others, I hope he dies!"

The man on the stairs was picking himself up. He looked down. A footman stood by the door leading to the servants' quarters.

"Put—put that gun down." Martin's voice was pitched low.

The man on the stairs levelled his gun, and was sideways to Martin for a split second. Martin's shot caught him on the wrist, and the gun dropped, fell over the banisters and hit the floor. The footman came running. Martin turned to the two girls, June in despair, Rhoda gloating.

"Please come," begged June.

"I hope he dies!" Rhoda screeched. "He—— "

Martin pushed past her, and June went with him into the room. Rhoda, silenced, followed quickly. Martin saw Grenfell lying on the floor with blood on his collar; a bullet had caught him in the side of the neck. He was conscious; even smiling tautly.

"Don't move!" June pleaded. "Martin—— "

"I'm all right," Grenfell muttered.

Martin said heavily, "Telephone for a doctor, June, and—— "

"I have."

"Oh. Good." Martin looked at Rhoda, and felt tired. There were jobs he hated, and, in a way, this was one. "Where's your gun, Rhoda?"

She started.

"*My* gun? Why—— "

Martin moved swiftly, knocked her handbag out of her hand, and dived his hand into the big pocket on the right side, and snatched out a gun.

"Thanks," he said. "You shot him. The man's bullet missed, I saw that. You followed me out, turned and shot him, when I was outside. Right, Grenfell?"

"Right," said Grenfell, as if the word hurt him.

Martin took Rhoda's arm as she began to rave. Tight in his grasp, she pulled to get free and screamed:

"And I'd shoot him again! He killed my mother, he killed Hilda. I'd shoot him a hundred times!"

"You won't," said Martin. "I—— "

He stopped, then pushed Rhoda with him, towards the landing.

The front door opened; obviously it had been on the latch. Reggie Fraser came in swiftly. Reggie reached the middle of the hall, as Rhoda was screaming; he heard every word. The footman switched on the main light, and it flooded the hall, staircase, and landing. It showed the ugly distortion of Rhoda's face and the tenseness of Fraser's.

The wounded man cried, " It's her fault, she really did it. She paid us to kill her mother, she—— "

Rhoda mouthed at him.

Martin let the girl go, then struck her on the side of the chin, as Fraser had done. She staggered, but he didn't knock her out.

Fraser came running.

" I'll hold her," he said.

Martin let him take her by the arm, and hold it behind her back; she couldn't move. The footman was bending over the helpless man on the stairs. Martin went back to the study. Grenfell was no longer smiling, but he was conscious, and badly hurt. June was on her knees beside him.

Someone near by, another servant, was calling desperately:

" Yes, hurry—hurry. I've given you the address. It's murder. A man's been shot. Hurry! "

He was telephoning the police.

Martin went into a bedroom for blankets, shouted to the servant for hot-water bottles, then returned to the study. June was holding the newspaper magnate's hand tightly, and seemed to have forgotten that Martin was here.

Grenfell smiled up at her suddenly, warmly. Martin could see how tightly he returned the girl's grip. Martin put blankets over the man as Grenfell spoke.

" I'm sorry you had to go through this, June. My own fault, really. Don't fret if I should die. Don't—— "

June said, " You mustn't talk. You're not going to die, but you'll make yourself worse if you don't lie quiet." She looked up.

" The police are on the way, they'll have a doctor," he said. " They may get here before the man you telephoned."

Grenfell was still smiling.

"Don't fight against it too hard, June. I'm afraid it's over. But you'll have everything you'll need."

She cried, "Oh, be quiet!" She swung round on Martin, and there were tears in her eyes. "Can't you hurry a doctor? Can't you keep him quiet? If he keeps on talking he'll kill himself."

"All right, June," Grenfell said. "I'm glad you're a fighter. I've always liked a fighter."

He lay quiet.

The girl straightened him, put a cushion under his head, and opened his shirt. She had padded the wound, too, with his own handkerchief; everything was done correctly. Now she stood looking down at the man, who smiled up. Once or twice his lips twisted, as with pain; but the smile came back.

Martin didn't do any guessing.

"Don't talk," he said. "Understand?"

Grenfell winked.

"I'll be back," said Martin. He went to the door, and heard voices downstairs and the sounds of several men coming in.

The police patrol car was here, but a doctor? Had he taken that too much for granted? He saw Fraser and Rhoda, on a couch on the landing. The girl leaned back with her eyes closed, all fury gone. She looked tired; older. So did Fraser, who stood up.

"I don't think there's any more fight in her," he said.

"Don't be too sure." Martin's voice was harsh. "Make sure she doesn't get away." He hurried down the stairs, where the footman, a maid, and several policemen were together, and the wounded man lay on the floor; it was like a battlefield.

"Ring the doctor again, please." He spoke to Webber.

"I told the police we would need one, they said he would be here straight away."

"One coming now," said a man bending over the gunman, and another man stepped briskly in.

"Not this chap first," Martin said. "Grenfell's hurt badly."

"I'll lead the way, sir." That was Webber. He went upstairs with the doctor, as a bulky Flying Squad man who had been bending over the gunman straightened up and came to Martin.

" You're Fane, aren't you ? "

" Yes."

" What's this about Sir Edward Grenfell ? "

" Much worse than this chap," said Martin. " Everything's laid on. Do you know who this is ? " He pointed to the wounded gunman.

" Slippy Lee."

" That's fine," said Martin softly. " I doubt if there are any others. You might try and make him talk before he gets stubborn—shock might loosen his tongue. Tell him Morris will give us the story, anyhow, and he might as well do what he can to help himself."

" What *is* this ? " The Squad man was on his way to the stairs, Martin by his side.

" Can't it wait for Kelby ? " asked Martin.

The other shrugged and looked down his nose.

" If you say so. I—what's *that* ? "

A shriek cut across his words, high-pitched, ear-splitting. On the landing, Rhoda Grenfell was on her feet, and screamed again. Fraser was staggering back from her. She turned and climbed on to the banisters. The drop to the hall below was all of twenty feet. She struggled to climb over, as Fraser recovered and rushed forward. Fraser could have held her, but he stopped abruptly. Martin saw his face, with all the misery in the world showing in it.

Rhoda jumped.

27   LIFE AND DEATH

" AND in spite of all that she didn't die," Fraser said thinly. " Just broke a leg."

It was two hours later, and they were at his flat.

They had spent an hour at the Yard, and had just arrived. He'd wanted to come alone, but Martin had been obstinate, and Richard had insisted on coming along. Now Richard

occupied himself by looking for the drinks.   Fraser watched
him sombrely.

" You know I let her jump, don't you ? "

Martin shrugged.   " Best not admitted."

" I don't care who knows.   If she'd killed herself it would
have been better for every one."

Richard had finished his hunt, successfully, and was
pouring out whiskies-and-soda.

" Possibly."   Martin put his pipe between his lips.
" I'm not sure.   Not better for you, for instance.   You'd
have had some silly notion that you'd helped her to
die."

" Better help her to die that way than help her to hang,"
said Fraser.   He looked at Richard still sombrely, but took
a proffered glass.   " Thanks."   He stopped.   Richard
went to a chair and sat on the arm.   " Martin, when did you
first think Rhoda was behind it ? "

" Hard to say," Martin muttered, sipped, and went on,
" It was always her or Grenfell.   I suppose Hilda's death
settled it.   Not the shooting at her—but poison."

" I wish I knew what started her on it," Fraser said.

" I doubt if we'll find out, unless Grenfell lives."   Grenfell, in hospital, was on the danger-list.   " She might talk
herself.   I can't explain motives, but it's clear that she set
out to kill them, one after the other, and to blame Grenfell
for it.   I don't know why she had a go at you.   No doubt
she had her mother killed ; no doubt she poisoned Hilda
after the first attempt had killed the chauffeur.   She was at
Nairn Lodge, the only one there with any possible motive for
poisoning Hilda, and I'm quite sure Hilda wasn't in suicidal
mood last night.   The thing that amazes me is that they let
Rhoda leave there."

Richard chimed in, " Kelby says they suspected her, and
wanted to give her plenty of rope.   Careless.   What the
Yard would do without us I really don't know ! "

Martin glared at him.   Richard shrugged.

Fraser said, " What else made you think it was
Rhoda ? "

" I think Grenfell found out.   That's probably why he
withdrew from the agency—a kind of family loyalty.   I
didn't tell you about that, did I ?   He said at first that

both his sister-in-law and Rhoda were in trouble and he wanted to find out why. He didn't think it was a police job, and preferred to keep it away from his newspapermen. He felt he could rely on Prince to keep it confidential. Then his sister-in-law was killed, and he asked us to solve that. Then I think he realised later who had killed her. He could either go on, hunting his own niece down, or sack us. He chose to sack us. But he couldn't have thought she would try to have him killed too."

"Why did she want Reggie killed?" asked Richard bluntly.

"I don't know," said Martin. "Do you, Reggie?"

"I think so," said Fraser slowly. "I went to her flat one day, and a man called. He said enough to make me wonder whether she was—good. I didn't know a thing, but I do now. The man was Slippy Lee. Rhoda probably thought I knew more than I did, so——" He broke off.

"Motive for attempted murder," Richard said. "I'm damned sorry, Reggie."

Fraser said, "I'm all right. Much rather be left on my own."

"We'll go," Martin decided.

Outside, in the mews, Richard said, "I'm not sure you were right, Scoop. If you'd jollied him a bit more it might have been better. Still, you're the Boss. More than ever, after this! Want me?"

"What do you want to do?"

"I might keep an eye on him," said Richard. "Type to do foolish things. If he stays in the flat for an hour I think he'll be all right."

Martin gripped his arm. "You stay," he said.

He drove off slowly, towards the Strand. It was bitterly cold, and the quicker he was at the flat the better. Barbara would be waiting to hear the story. He must telephone to Nairn Lodge, too. He drove to the flat. The light was on in the big front room, and as he reached the flat door, it opened. Barbara was there.

It was always comforting to be with Barbara. She didn't say much. The electric fire was on, and a kettle was singing. She had cut sandwiches. He sat back, eyes closed, and was listening to her moving about the kitchen, when the telephone bell rang.

Barbara called, " I'll answer it ! "

" I'm nearest," said Martin. He picked up the receiver as Barbara appeared in the doorway. " Hallo ? "

" Oh, Mr. Martin." It was Jessica. " I thought I ought to tell you that Mr. Wimple asked me again, so I did what you told me."

" And what did Mr. Wimple want ? " asked Martin. He noticed it wasn't " that man " or " that cop ".

" Nothing," said Jessica. " That is, *nothing* about Prince. But I thought I ought to tell you, right away."

Martin found himself smiling. " That's fine," he said. " Thanks, Jessica." He put down the receiver, told Barbara, and wondered if the Yard man was falling in love with an old lag's daughter. It might be an advantage to have a regular C.I.D. man on the fringe of the family. He chuckled aloud ; he was feeling much better, the nonsensical idea of closing up Prince was already gone.

Barbara came in with sandwiches and coffee.

" That's much better," she said. " Now tell me all about it."

.   .   .   .   .

Grenfell didn't die.

His statements to the police, added to Slippy Lee's, helped to piece the story together. It had started a long while before. In the gay days Rhoda had spent wildly, lost heavily at the gaming-tables, found herself deeply in debt. She had been desperate when she got on to Hilda Kennedy. There was no doubt that it was Rhoda who had the hold on Hilda. She had found the proof that Fraser had been looking for—proof that Hilda was a fraud and a cheat. First she had blackmailed Hilda—bled her white, in fact ; then she had forced Hilda to join in her other money-raising schemes.

One of these was the blackmailing of Grenfell. Rhoda did it through Hilda—and in such a way that Grenfell guessed that Hilda was behind it. That was to divert suspicion from herself. Then Hilda had to try to get money out of Rhoda's mother, by warnings and messages from the stars. But Rhoda's mother didn't fall for that, so in the end Rhoda decided to kill her and get the money that way. Again she was going to drag Hilda into it—not frame her, exactly, but leave a way clear for her to throw suspicion on the older woman if she herself were in danger.

But then Grenfell had come into the picture.

Rhoda had been keeping a watch on him, through Lee. Grenfell had spoken the truth when he said that he had called at Prince twice before, in the evening, and found the office closed. Slippy had followed him, and reported to Rhoda. She saw her chance, and made her appointment for the next evening, just before the time she expected Grenfell to arrive. She forestalled him by seeing Martin herself first, sowing the seeds of suspicion against her uncle— and making it appear as if he had been following her to the agency. Then she had her mother murdered, with strong suspicion already planted against Grenfell.

" Of course," Martin told Richard, " her build-up of her relations with Hilda was brilliantly clever. Every one, her mother and her uncle included, thought that Hilda was her evil genius, instead of the other way round. And she made us think that, too. Remember that business at Hilda's flat, on the first evening? And then the next day she made me even surer that Hilda was dominating her by the oldest dodge in the world—assuring me indignantly that Hilda was *not* dominating her !

" I never saw through that until we were down at the Maestro's, and Hilda went to her room that night. The masks were off then—Hilda was too scared for her own skin to be able to act, even if she tried. But Rhoda got her out too quickly for me to be really sure. And the next day she got rid of her for ever."

The rest was straightforward. Rhoda had started by using Prince for her own ends—to divert suspicion to her uncle and, to a lesser extent, to Hilda. She had had the Fanes attacked in their flat partly to find out what Grenfell had said to them, but especially to make it appear that the attackers were hired by Grenfell and working against Rhoda. The phone call to Jonathan Fane was made with the same intention.

Later she wished she had not brought Prince into it, and

tried to get them out again by getting Slippy Lee to tip off the Yard that Richard had been present at the murder of her mother. When Richard was released from Scotland Yard, she decided that the Fanes must be killed as well.

Hilda had begun to crack long before then. She had guessed that Rhoda had killed her mother, and was liable to break down and tell the police everything. So Rhoda decided to kill her.

When Martin had left her at the flat, she had telephoned Hilda, telling her to follow her to Dorset; then she had spoken to Slippy Lee, planning Hilda's murder. When the chauffeur died and Hilda lived, she poisoned Hilda, who, if she turned against her, could have damned Rhoda. She had poison tablets in an aspirin bottle which she always carried with her, to kill herself if she were caught. When she had needed them, Martin had knocked her bag out of her hand.

Then Rhoda became sure that Grenfell had realised the truth. If only she could blame Grenfell for it all, she saw an illusory safety for herself. She telephoned him, and he said enough to make her sure that he was aware of her guilt. She didn't think he would work against her, but wasn't sure. She begged for time—and laid more plans.

She thought she was free from suspicion, as the police let her leave Nairn Lodge. She planned the attack on Fraser, and when that failed, made a final desperate attempt to save herself.

Lee, now completely in her power—for if she were caught she could have his guilt proved—was to go and kill Grenfell. She laid the trail for Martin and Richard to go to Grenfell's house. She wanted to put up a show of angry innocence, while distracting the Fanes' attention from Slippy.

She failed, again, and tried to kill Grenfell, to silence him. Even the police admitted that she might have got away with that, for a while, but for Martin.

Reggie had been Rhoda's third string. She knew about his past, but never tried to blackmail him; she had just kept him handy as another suspect if she needed one. His background fitted him for the rôle.

The Fanes learned all that—and still didn't know for

certain what Rhoda had known about Grenfell, so that she could blackmail him.

It wasn't until Grenfell was out of hospital that they learned that.

.   .   .   .   .

Grenfell was sitting up in an easy-chair in his study, on a bright spring afternoon; convalescing. June was there, with Martin and Richard and Jonathan Fane. He smiled faintly when Jonathan said :

" Now tell us the truth, and stop us guessing. What's your dreadful secret ? "

Grenfell said quietly, " You've guessed June is my daughter, of course."

" Why keep that a secret after your wife died ? Forgive my bluntness." Fane's voice was gentle.

" I'd kept it secret during my wife's life," Grenfell said quietly, " and—it became a skeleton. I don't know how Rhoda discovered it, but she worked on it cleverly. I'd done what I could for June, of course, after handing her over to her foster-parents for years, but it was—impersonal. The blackmailing started during my wife's lifetime. After my wife died, I brought June on to the *Clarion* staff, and eventually made her one of my secretaries." He glanced at June. " I've never had a better. She didn't know the truth, of course. And now it's all in the open."

June didn't speak ; but smiled, and her smile was very like his. So was her composure.

" The blackmailing wasn't really serious until a month or two ago, when the demands increased sharply. You know the rest. Is it worth putting in a book ? "

" Oh, the Maestro would improve on it," said Richard. " You'd have a murder or two in your past."

Grenfell scowled.

" June's told me you wanted to influence my business your way."

" When shall we sign the contract ? " asked Richard.

Grenfell chuckled.

" Ask June to have a draft prepared ! Now—nothing needs repeating, does it ? You know Rhoda discovered that I was going to use Prince, and decided to try to forestall me by getting in first. You know, Fane, I hadn't realised before what a disadvantage you whodunit merchants work under. You have to have everything sewn up, tight and logical, don't you? Even to making Rhoda credible. Don't ask me to explain how she got into it, what twisted her mind so that she started to kill and then had to keep on. Don't try to explain it to me, either! I—— "

There was a tap at the door.

" Come in."

A footman opened the door and stood aside. " Mr. Fraser, sir."

Fraser came in. Martin saw June's face light up, Richard smothered a grin, Jonathan Fane promptly decided that it was time they were going. Fraser and June saw them to the front door.

" Not much doubt what's developing there," said Jonathan Fane. " Nothing in the open until after the trials, of course. Slippy Lee and Rhoda will hang. Haven't a chance to escape. Almost a good thing Morris died, he cheated the gallows."

" First time I knew you were against capital punishment," said Martin.

" Oh, I'm not. In principle, that is. Hate the thought of hanging, all the time. Not civilised. Never mind." Fane smiled, suddenly. " I must get back, I promised your mother I'd be home in time for dinner, and I'm driving myself. She wanted me to bring Sampson—— "

" Is he really fit? " asked Richard quickly.

" Never been fitter. Laughs about the crack over the head." Fane got into his car, which was parked behind his sons' Buick. " No, I mustn't be late. There's one good thing about this case, your mother was wrong about Rhoda. She quite liked the girl! " He shrugged. " So we can't take anything for granted. Think you'll get that contract with the *Clarion*? "

" It's in the bag," said Richard.

" Long life to Prince, then," said Jonathan Fane. " Your mother will get reconciled to it one of these days, but keep your murders out of Dorset, will you? "

" Sorry, Maestro," said Richard humbly.

Fane chuckled. " You'll do. I wouldn't see you out of

that business for the world.   By the way, young Wimple was in the office this morning, talking to Jessica.   She was chattering nineteen to the dozen, and not blushing.   What's happening ? "

'Nothing you'd disapprove of," Richard assured him.

He stood with Martin on the kerb as Fane drove off.